I0690601

MEN IN PERIL

First Edition

Published by The Nazca Plains Corporation
Las Vegas, Nevada
2010

ISBN: 978-1-935509-87-5

Published by

The Nazca Plains Corporation ®
4640 Paradise Rd, Suite 141
Las Vegas NV 89109-8000

PUBLISHER'S NOTE
Men in Peril is a work of fiction created wholly by *Christopher Trevor's* imagination. All characters are fictional and any resemblance to any persons living or deceased is purely by accident. No portion of this book reflects any real person or events.

Male Cover Photo, Francesco Cura
Art Director, Blake Stephens

DEDICATION

Eden, I'm glad you are back in my life...

MEN IN PERIL

First Edition

Christopher Trevor

CONTENTS

INTRODUCTION

What exactly is a man in peril? When exactly is a man in peril? Before anyone can answer those questions what first must be defined is what sort of peril do men find themselves in? Of course the scenarios of when a man finds himself in peril can be endless. A man can be in peril where his life is actually in danger; he can be in career peril, which could lead to financial peril, which could lead to relationship peril, etc... But for the purposes of this book I have put men in what I call erotic peril. The stories you will find in this latest publication center around police officer abduction, rookie cop abduction, an executive finds himself in some sexy peril when he foolishly agrees to a game of chance with two of his underlings while on a business trip and no book of mine about "Men In Peril" would be complete without at least a couple of appearances by my two recurring sadistic characters, those relentless kidnappers, Cleeve and Otis.

When I had decided on an assortment of stories that would focus on "Men In Peril" I asked some of my erotic reading and writing buddies for their definitions of what they thought were "Men In Peril." The replies I received varied yet had the common denominators of the scenarios of domination and submission, these two basic instincts factoring hotly in what defines a man in peril.

My recurring ticklish character Timmy Backman (tickle star of my books "Timmy's Ticklish Trials, Timmy and the Hong Kong Tailor, Timmy and the Evil Dr. Von Vellicator and a host of other tickle books) constantly finds himself in tickle peril. His personal definition of a "Man In Peril" is the following:

> *For me, "Men In Peril" centers on discipline, humiliation, embarrassment, and almost always has to include a sexual aspect which is almost always non-consensual or contrary to the will of the man who is in peril. I am a tickle-file and love to see men being subdued and dominated through tickling. But spanking, public stripping and dressing downs, sexual teasing, orgasm/cum control are also things I dream of when I think of myself or other men in peril. What are they in peril of really? They are in peril of being sexually dominated and will suffer the stinging humiliations of a spanking or public stripping, or perhaps having their sexual release controlled by others and totally contrary to their own will. I truly look forward to reading what Christopher Trevor has put together to describe his "Men In Peril."*

> *- Timmy Backman-*

For my long-time internet buddy Joe A. "Men In Peril" center on the entertainment arena.

Joe's definition of "Men In Peril" is:

> *My idea of "Men In Peril" come from the movies and the comics- in old serials like Flash Gordon or when some other super hero usually ended up captured and tied up by the villain. These scenes have always had a very strong homoerotic subtext. The handsome, usually shirtless man finds himself at the mercy of some diabolical contraption. The villain might not be overtly Gay but the threat of rape, which is a real plight for any "Man In Peril", was always implied.*

Fellow author Ron Bossman sums up "Men In Peril" this way:

> *What often comes to mind when thinking of a man in peril is someone hanging by his fingertips on the edge of a cliff or perhaps crossing an alligator infested river in order to get back to civilization. What comes to my mind is a bit different. I picture men who have been captured, trapped, or perhaps even coerced ever so subtly into submission. The act of capturing or trapping a man isn't always very difficult. It could be just a simple act of blackmail. The peril enters the equation when the man starts to enjoy the act. When the evidence of that enjoyment shows up through arousal, yes, an erection is what I am referring to here, that my friends is the true definition of a man in peril.*

A reader of my more hardcore works, a gentleman named Bob defines "Men In Peril" this way:

> *"Men In Peril" to me are men who have no control over their current circumstances and are at the whims and mercy of their captor/dominator...much like Christopher Trevor does in his infamous "Cleeve and Otis" tales.*

Reader turned writer Sean Scriber defines a man in peril this way:

> *First of all I cannot wait to read this book. My personal definition of a man in peril would be a man whose personal body or integrity is threatened by someone else. In an erotic sense, a man's body could be abused or he could be forced to respond when he doesn't want it to be so. One other scenario is that a man's integrity could be endangered. For example, a man could be forced to betray his wedding vows or even be seduced into breaking other promises...*

A reviewer of my books on AMAZON.com, a gentleman I recently even had the pleasure of meeting in person summed up "Men In Peril" this way:

> *What would define for me a man in peril? Hmm, someone tied up and forced to listen to someone reading them the*

BIBLE (or the Republican's manifesto) is the most horrifying thing I can think of.

Seriously though, beaten, raped, forcibly milked and NOT allowed to cum, perhaps gang-tickled by about fifteen guys, short of bloodletting, amputation and murder (which I don't think anyone would want to read about in a Christopher Trevor book, except maybe the criminally insane.) Theses are as perilous of situations for men that I can think of.

And finally, to sum it all up for "Men In Peril", fellow author and friend, Nick Bowman offers his most diabolical scenario in the following litany:

What is a man in peril? Where is a man in peril?

New moon at perigee streets are dark, tides rough and danger is high.

Is that soft sharp sound someone coming or just the wind scraping an old paper along the ground? Is that sudden move someone grabbing someone or just a cat jumping onto a fence?

Then: an arm around the neck; another presses the head forward. Ninety seconds before blackout. A stomp to the instep- a back-fist to the groin- a turn of the head into the crook of the elbow- to no avail. Things blur to grey, then black. Consciousness slips away.

What is a man in peril? When is a man in peril?

Consciousness returns with the scents of piss, shit and sweat. But also comes the awareness of being naked, tied up, legs splayed, cock and balls dangling, all exposed and unguarded, totally accessible.

The ropes are rough, tight, and secure. The seat of the chair is hard, worn smooth and U-shaped.

Nipples are dark, taut nubs from the cold. Hole is clenched, braced for assault. The sac smails and thickens around the testicles. Arousal is as much from fear as desire.

What is a man in peril? Why is a man in peril?

The room reveals nothing: cement floor, worn brick walls, a single industrial pendant dangling from the ceiling. The heat from the bulb warms the top of the head.

Somewhere, from behind, a door creaks open. A dark, deep chuckle is heard. Cold flickers along tight abs and footsteps echo. The door clangs shut and a hand rests on the shoulder. A sidelong glance sees it is covered with a supple black leather glove.

The answer to the unasked question comes to mind. Even if it is possible to get out alive, it may not be in one piece, and cock and resolve stiffen.

What is a man in peril? Who is a man in peril???

A Boner Book

JIMMY'S STORY

"I can't believe you just told us that man!!" my buddy Frank said to me with a look of outright disgust on his face.

"Me either," my other buddy Richie chimed in. "You mean to tell us that you have a faggot for a roommate and you let him lick your sweaty socks and mangy briefs at the end of the day…*while you're wearing them???*"

I nodded yes with a big shit eating grin on my face as I sat on the floor and leaned against the wall in the hallway where my two buddies and I were working that day. I had propped my big size eleven construction booted feet in front of myself. I went on to tell my two buddies of how my gay roommate also sucks my dick everyday, once in the morning and once at night, adding how the guy swallows and chugs down my cum…and on occasion he will even drink my goddamned piss. My two buddies looked even more disgusted by all that, and yet, somehow intrigued at the same time.

My name is Jimmy. My two good buddies (Richie and Frank) and I work for a seasonal construction company called Green's and Sons. On the day that I'm telling you about we had been sent over to an office building on the upper west side of Manhattan to renovate an entire floor. We had begun work at seven AM and at twelve PM stopped for a much needed lunch break. It was summer time, ninety degrees with one hundred percent humidity. Because all the power was turned off on the floor we were working on all three of us were a sweaty stinking mess of guys when we sat down on the floor to eat. As Richie gulped a cold can of soda he made a comment on how bad his underwear and socks smell at the end of the day. So bad that his wife won't handle them. He has to put them in the washing machine himself. Don't ask me what made Richie suddenly mention his stinking socks and underwear, I suppose it's just a guy thing. But that was when, seeing as we had embarked on a conversation about sleazy guy things, I told them about Brad...Brad, my gay and extremely raunchy roommate.

"And every fucking night he licks and sucks the juice out of your stinking briefs and socks?" Richie asked me again in awe.

"Sure does, which is why I always wear these thin dress socks all the time," I replied, hiking up my worn blue Levis jeans, revealing the tops of my thin blue dress socks. "At the end of a hot workday these socks stink one hundred times worse than those thick sweat socks you guys wear. And believe me, poor Brad suffers through licking them. I even make the mangy faggot roll them off me and then lick my bare feet."

"OHHHHHH man, now that is too much," Frank moaned with a fiendish looking smile on his face.

"You know, I always did wonder why you wore those thin dressy socks," Richie said, moving next to me.

He placed a hand around the top of one of my blue socks which was sticking out of my size eleven mustard colored construction boot.

"There is something kinky and raunchy about it," Richie said, toying with my sock and looking over at Frank. "I mean a construction dude in thin dress socks and construction boots? Sure is sweaty raunchy to me man."

"How did this shit with your faggot roommate get started?" Frank asked me and took a bight of his hero sandwich.

"I'll tell you…" I said as Richie continued toying with my sock, snapping the elastic of it against my skin.

I moved to New York from Washington three years ago when I was twenty-three years old. I took a room in YMCA while I apartment hunted. When I saw how much the rents in New York were, I realized that my job with Green and Son's was not going to pay those kinds of rents. So I decided to try and find a roommate. I registered with a roommate service and thankfully, within two weeks I had found a beautiful apartment and a roommate named Brad. Even before I moved in Brad told me he was gay. He was real honest and upfront this guy. I told him that that didn't bother me in the least. When I told him I was straight, he told me that that didn't bother him in the least. We both laughed at our comments and became instant buddies. Brad works in a bank as some sort of manager, which means a suit and tie every fucking day. He's the same age I am. He has yellow blond hair, dark blue eyes, and a lean yet muscular body. I have jet black hair, dark eyes, and a very muscular body from what I do for a living as a construction worker. A few times after I was done showering I caught Brad looking at me as I walked to my room wearing just a towel. It didn't bother me at all…in fact I was sort of flattered by the faggot's admiration of my body. One day when it was particularly hot I got home early from work (around three thirty PM) and found one of Brad's gay magazines on the coffee table. I stripped down to my white briefs and white sweat socks and curious about the magazine I sat down on the couch, propping my smelly socked feet up on the coffee table. I picked up the magazine. It was called "Foot Scene…" a magazine strictly devoted to male foot fetishism. I couldn't believe it, an entire magazine devoted to men's feet. As I skimmed through the pages I saw pictures of guys licking other guy's feet and even sucking on their goddamned toes. Some of the guys having their feet worked on were still wearing their socks. Other pictures were of guys wearing construction boots with a guy licking and kissing their boots. At first I was appalled by it all, I nearly threw the magazine across the room. But then I got to thinking how it would probably feel really great at the end of a long workday to have someone lick my tired and hot feet…not to mention raunchy smelling. I looked down at my big socked feet and imagined Brad kneeling there, servicing them…

"Fucking Brad…" I mused with a grin on my face. "Fuckin' foot lovin' faggot…"

As I thought about it, I wondered just what besides raunchy feet would excite Brad. But then, my thoughts were cut short as Brad came into the apartment. Coincidentally he also came home early from work that day. As he walked in I quickly threw the magazine down on the couch. Too late though because Brad had seen what I was looking at.

"Hey, you're home early too," Brad said, stepping in front of the coffee table where my feet were still propped. "Too hot to work out in the heat huh?"

"Yeah, too hot…" I replied. "Why are you home early?"

"Air conditioning went out in my office," Brad said, loosening his tie. "They let everyone go home early."

"Uh-huh," I said slowly as Brad squatted by the coffee table.

He picked up the foot fetish magazine and looked at me.

"Interesting stuff huh?" he asked me with a grin.

GAWD, his face was practically right next to my damned stinking feet. My heart was pounding like crazy.

"Yeah, interesting," I said to him. "You, uh, you're into all that…I mean, uh…"

Smiling, Brad put the magazine down and looked at my feet.

"Just relax Jimmy," Brad whispered and pressed his nose and lips against the bottom of one of my feet.

"B-Brad…no…" I whispered, but not really meaning it.

"Mmm…just as I thought…" Brad murmured. "Nice and funky smelling."

I watched in awe as Brad inhaled the aroma of my sweaty stinky socks. The guy had a look of pure ecstasy on his face as he kissed and sniffed both my feet all over, he sucked at my toes through my socks, dribbled and licked saliva onto and off my stinking socks.

"OHHHH shit, that feels great…" I said breathlessly.

As Brad worked on my socked feet my dick grew long and hard in my sweaty briefs. There was no denying it…I was totally turned on by the faggot servicing my damned feet.

"Since you moved in here I've wanted to do this Jimmy," Brad said, looking up at me with his hands around my ankles and holding them tight. "Your feet are so big…and so beautiful. And judging from that boner in your briefs you're not so turned off by it at all."

I looked at him and then sneered as mean looking as possible.

"Fucking foot lover!!" I snapped at him. "Get those rancid socks off my goddamned feet and lick my feet bare…NOW!!"

I really got into character at that moment let me tell you. Playing his part, Brad slowly rolled my stinky sweat socks off my feet and proceeded to service my bare and very smelly feet with his lips and tongue.

"OHHHHHH yeah, that feels so fucking good at the end of a hard day," I moaned as I rubbed the boner in my briefs. "If you do a real good job on my feet I'll give you this hard-on to service next. Does that sound good you foot faggot?"

"It sure does," Brad said and slurped one of my big toes into his eager mouth.

He sucked my toes like they were dicks. The fucking guy was driving me batty and all he was doing was licking and sucking my damned feet. A little while later, after my feet were thoroughly cleaned and smelling fresh, I stood rigidly still as the fucker knelt in front of me and ran that hot tongue of his all over my sweat soaked mangy briefs.

"Fucking raunchy guy you are," I whispered as Brad licked and sucked the cotton material of my white briefs.

He pressed his mouth against my ass and nipped it a few times through my briefs. He had not yet touched my hard-on with his mouth. I got to tell you guys, my cock was oozing pre cum like crazy, right through the front of my goddamned briefs. But then, oh man then, the faggot pursed his lips and sucked that pre cum right off my briefs and gulped it down.

"OHHHHHHH fuck," I moaned. "Fuckin' driving me crazy…"

Slowly, Brad pulled my briefs off me and my thick, hard, nine inch dick was jutting out in front of me like a goddamned flagpole.

"Oh God," Brad said in awe as he stared at my monster sized manhood.

It was throbbing with a life of it's own as more and more pre cum dripped out of it. I tell you guys, I never thought that having a faggot worship my damned feet could have gotten me so worked up in the crotch. My big balls were hanging low in my sweaty smelling sac; they were filled to overflowing with my creamy white man juice. I nearly jumped through the ceiling when Brad kissed my balls. Then, with his hands on my thighs he gobbled my dick into his mouth and began sucking me like crazy. His tongue darted in and out of my piss hole a few times. That felt like magic and really sent me into a goddamned frenzy. I stood there sweating all over again as Brad sucked my meat like no girl ever did. I gyrated my hips involuntarily as Brad sucked my throbbing dick as deep into his throat as he could get it. I grunted that I was about to cum but Brad just kept my dick in his mouth. The faggot gulped down my juices as I roared like an animal in heat and shot what seemed like an endless amount of jizz into his mouth. Brad scoffed it all down as fast as possible. When I was done and trying to catch my breath Brad continued sucking my dick. Now I don't know about you guys but after I've shot a big creamy load my dick is super sensitive and I don't want anyone touching it. But now, my super sensitive dick was trapped in the fucker's mouth and he was still sucking it.

"GAWD, no, OHHHHHH BRAD," I roared as my head spun. "B-Brad, y-you're going to make me…piss…ohhhhhhhhh shit…"

It's what he wanted. He made me piss into his mouth and he swallowed all that too. When I was done pissing, I sat back down on the couch to catch my breath all over again. Brad looked at me in an uncertain way as I propped my bare feet back up on the coffee table.

"You're not mad at me are you Jimmy?" Brad asked me, looking at my feet again.

"Mad?" I asked him. "Hell no. In fact, I just came up with a great idea…"

A few minutes later I was wearing Brad's black dress socks that he had worn for work that day on my feet and he was kneeling before *my feet*…licking *his* socks clean.

"OHHHH yeah, feels so fucking good," I said breathlessly. "From now on Brad you'll be servicing my socks and feet every night when I get home from work…and if you do a good job I'll let you have my dick juice as a bonus."

Well, as you can imagine Brad always does a good job cleaning my socks and then my feet…so he always gets my dick juice. Right after that first time that Brad serviced my feet, I went to a shoe store and bought him dress socks…a lot of pairs…in all different colors…

My story finished, I looked across at Frank. Richie was still sitting next to me, toying with my sock.

"So, what do you guys think?" I asked them with a grin.

Richie snapped the elastic in my sock and smiled over at Frank.

A few moments later my construction boots were off my feet and my two buddies were each licking, sucking, and kissing my feet. My story had worked. I had always wanted Richie and Frank to service my feet… I leaned back and enjoyed…

OFFICER ROMANO AND THE THEATER OF HELL

Prologue

Before I begin to tell you about the most harrowing night of my life let me first tell you some stuff about me and Perry Banks. My name is John Romano. I am a New York City police officer, have been for the past seven years. I'm a muscular, six foot tall Italian dude with a thick mustache. What I'm going to tell you about happened three years ago at this point. It took me that long to be able to get up the nerve to write it all down. But yes, first Perry Banks…

Perry was wannabe actor, make-up artist, master of disguises, and a crook. He used his genius with make-up and disguises to pull off a string of robberies in New York City. When he held up the first jewelry store he disguised himself as a rabbi. When he robbed an electronics store he disguised himself as an eighties punk rocker. When he robbed the second jewelry store he made himself up as a woman. When he held up the owner of a decorating center, he was disguised as a priest, complete with a fake mustache and old-fashioned bifocal glasses. The night he held up a twenty-four hour grocery store I was there. I was off duty and heading home for the night. I was wearing civilian clothing and had stopped in to the store to buy some odds and ends. As I browsed around I saw a man dressed as a cowboy enter the store and point a gun at the man behind the counter. The cowboy ordered the guy behind the counter to give him all the money that was in the cash register, him not knowing that anyone else was in the store…let alone an off duty police officer. Silently, I crept up behind the cowboy, motioning to the guy behind the counter to remain silent. I was unarmed and would only have one chance. When I was close enough I yelled, "Hey You!" at the cowboy's back. As he turned around I kicked the gun out of his hand and followed up with another karate style kick to his stomach area. We were about the same height and he went down in a heap, gasping for air. The guy behind the counter stood riveted to the spot as I picked up Perry's gun and tucked it into the waistband of my pants. I showed the guy my badge and told him to call the police. The man on the floor tried to get up but I punched him twice in the face, flooring him again. I told him that he was under arrest and read him his rights. Two of my police buddies showed up to take the cowboy into custody. He was charged with armed robbery and possession of an illegal weapon.

The next day I found out that Perry Banks had confessed to all of the other robberies I mentioned earlier. When his apartment was searched my cop buddies and I found all sorts of costumes, disguises, make-up, and a host of other actor's accessories. The mayor of New York proclaimed me a hero for being in the right place at the right time and for being so brave. At Perry's trial his lawyer defended him by arguing that Perry was a troubled man who desperately wanted to be an actor. The prosecution tagged him a common criminal and a menace to society. The jury came back with a verdict of "Guilty." On the day of Perry's sentencing I was present in the courtroom and listened as the judge sentenced him to four years in prison, eligible for parole in two years. Perry simply stood there wearing a brown suit, his head hanging down. Out of costume Perry was a tall, brown haired man. As Perry was led out of the courtroom in handcuffs he happened to see me standing there in my dark blue police uniform. Our eyes made contact for a split second or so and then he was taken away.

Perry served his first two years in prison and he was granted parole. I could not believe it, but I accepted it as I had no control over it. Perry committed his last and biggest robbery while he was out on parole. You see, Perry stole me. Actually, the bastard kidnapped me (right off my beat) and held me prisoner and tortured me for about twelve horrible hours. They were the very worst twelve hours of my life and I was put through tortures and trials that no man should ever have to endure…

It was a Saturday night around nine o'clock. I was walking foot beat in Downtown Brooklyn. I had just walked past a closed down and abandoned movie theater when an old man came hobbling up behind me.

"Officer, Officer, please help me," he panted.

I turned and saw a man of about seventy to seventy-five years old, all wrinkled and stooped over standing in front of me.

"What's the problem Sir?" I asked him as he stood there wheezing.

Pointing at the theater I had just walked past he told me that his wife suffered from Alzheimer's disease and that she had wandered into that building. When he had gone in after her she was laying at the bottom of a flight of stairs, unconscious. He went on to tell me that he had covered her up with a curtain that he had found in there to keep her warm until he could bring help.

"Please, *please help her,*" the old man begged. "Please Officer…"

Without thinking I went into the theater with the old man trailing behind me.

"Can't believe this door was open…" I said as I walked into the front entrance of the theater. "More than likely some punks broke in here to use the place for drug deals…"

The lights from the street lit my way to the flight of stairs that the old man had told me about.

"She's down there," he said, pointing with a trembling finger.

I noticed how much wrinkled his hand was. I took my flashlight off my duty-belt, clicked it on, and shone it down the stairs. I saw what looked like a body under a curtain. I rushed down, followed by the old man. I should have realized that the old man was now moving as fast as I was down those stairs but I was mostly concerned with the woman under the curtain. I squatted down on my haunches and pulled the curtain off the body. Under the curtain was a mannequin.

"Hey, what the fuck is this?!?" I yelled.

I turned to look at the old man. He was standing over me with a spray can pointed directly at my face. Before I could think to do anything he sprayed the contents of the spray can directly in my face. It smelled like ether or something like it. I fell back onto the floor in a stupor. As I reached for my gun in its holster the old man fell on me and quickly pressed a rag that was scented/soaked with the same stuff that was in the spray can against my nose and mouth. In the stupor I had been sprayed into there wasn't much I could do to defend myself as unconsciousness claimed me.

When I came to an hour or so later (by my best estimates) the theater was flooded with light. I looked around and was shocked at where I found myself to be *and* the position that I was in. I was sitting on a wooden straight backed chair on a stage of the theater. My hands were cuffed behind me (with my own handcuffs mind you) and to the chair. My legs were spread and my feet were each securely tied to one of the legs of the chair each with mounds of tightly knotted rope. I was wearing only my white Jockey brand under shorts, my navy blue knee length socks, and my black police issued lace-up shoes. My dick and balls were humiliatingly hanging out of the fly opening of my under shorts and I nearly shrieked when I saw that there were thin wires with electrodes wrapped around my nuts. Electrodes were also clipped to my big meaty nipples. The wires were all attached to a small metal box on the floor.

"Welcome Officer Romano!" a male voice said to me. "You are about to become the star of this old theater by starring in your own show...titled... *"Death of a Policeman."*

I looked around and saw the old man sitting in the first row of seats in the audience's section of the theater. My uniform was on the seat next to him. My duty-belt, along with my gun was on the other side of him.

"What the fuck is going on?!?" I roared. *"Who the fuck are you???"*

The old man stood up and peeled off his fake beard and wrinkled skin.

"Perry Banks!!" I yelled. "FUCK, *this is a goddamned outrage!"*

He simply laughed.

"You're a natural," he snickered when he'd stopped laughing and applauded.

Slowly, he climbed the steps to the stage and stood looming over me.

"I have waited two years for this moment Officer Romano," he said menacingly. "Now I will have my revenge. But before you die I want you to experience some of what I experienced in prison, along with some of my own creativity thrown in for your benefit. Do you have any idea what those convicts do to a handsome actor such as myself in prison???"

He picked up the box and placed his fingertip on the small lever. I suddenly knew what the wires and electrodes on my dick, balls and nipples were for.

"Jesus God, no!!!" I yelped. *"Don't do this Perry!!!"*

A smile of insanity formed on his lips.

"It really does my heart good to see you beg Cop!" Perry taunted me and began pushing the lever on the box slowly upward.

At first I felt a slight tingling in my nuts and nipples, but then it started getting really painful. It felt like my balls and nipples were literally being fried. As he moved the lever further up on the box I felt as if my body was being consumed by volts of electricity. I couldn't help it; I screamed in agony and squirmed miserably in the chair.

"Arrrrrghhhhhhhh!!!!" I roared in a pain I had never planned on experiencing. "Perry, they did not do this to you in prison!!"

"No, as I said some of this is my own creativity, and I just thought how much fun it would be for me to do it to you Cop…" Perry replied mockingly.

When the lever was all the way at the top of the box I looked down at my nipples. They were red and swollen. Actually, they looked as if they were about to burst. I screamed louder in a man's agony. My balls were also swollen but I couldn't bear to look at them. They felt as if they were the size of tennis balls.

"P-Perry, you'll hang for this!!" I yelled.

"No I won't, you will," he cackled.

I writhed in utter agony on the chair as the volts of electricity cooked my nipples and balls. Finally, Perry began pulling the lever down on the box. The pain slowly subsided. When the lever was halfway down the bastard pushed it back up again.

"AYYYYYYY!!!" I cried.

"Just kidding," Perry said.

Then, all at once he pulled the lever all the way down and put the box down. I hung my head and gasped for breath. Perry came over to me and took the wires and electrodes off my nuts and nipples. I looked up at him.

"Perry, you've kidnapped me!" I began breathlessly. "Abducting an officer of the law is a federal crime. You'll go back to prison…for life this time…"

"No I won't," he replied as he squeezed one of my nipples after taking the electrode off it, getting a moan out of me. "Because by the time you're found dead I'll be long gone."

I gulped hard in terror after hearing those words. The bastard planned on not just torturing me but murdering me too. Then, he pulled the ether soaked cloth from his pocket and slammed it against my face again. Once again a fitful sleep claimed me.

When I came to again I was hanging by my wrists from the ceiling way up above the stage. Perry had hooked me up to the rope that brought the curtain up and down. My feet were tied to a heavy sandbag on the floor. Perry was standing nearby next to a table on wheels. On the table was a roll of duct tape, a bottle of water, a can of shaving cream and mean looking sharp straight razor.

"What now???" I roared angrily.

Perry came over to me, wheeling the table with him.

"I'm going to give you the most painful shave of your stinking life Pig!" he said, slapping me hard across the face a few times.

"UHHFFFFF!!!" I panted as he slapped me.

I watched in agony as Perry pulled my under shorts down to my socked ankles.

"You have a skid-mark in those shorts Cop," he teased me.

Being Italian I have pretty thick hair on most parts of my muscular body, especially my crotch area and in my armpits. Those were the two areas that Perry was planning on concentrating on. My under shorts were down around my bound ankles and Perry teasingly pulled on my black pubic hair.

"Perfect," he said contentedly.

He stepped behind me and also commented approvingly on my hairy butt, giving it two hard slaps, one on each muscular cheek. I was mortified and seething with anger at this point. I wanted to kill him. But in the position I was in I was totally helpless. Perry picked up the duct tape and began wrapping it around my crotch and butt. My heart pounded in fear because I knew what the guy was about to do to me. Once my crotch area was covered in duct tape Perry began pulling it off me, pulling my hair off my crotch at the same time.

"ARRRRRR!!! YOU SICK BASTARD!!!" I screamed at him.

When all the tape was off me the sticky side of it was covered with my hair. I thanked God that Perry hadn't stuck the duct tape on my exposed dick. Perry went to work on my hairy and bushy armpits next. He stuck a piece of duct tape onto each of my armpits and yanked it off and put it back again, over and over and over. I screamed like a caged animal as the hair was pulled painfully from my poor pits. What remained of the hair on my crotch and armpits Perry soaked with warm water and then sprayed shaving cream onto it. Helpless, I watched as he used the sharp straight razor to shave the hair off my crotch and balls and my armpits. A few times he purposely nicked me, causing me to yell out in pain. When Perry was done he placed the razor against my throat.

"I should kill you now…" he said threateningly, pressing the razor against my Adam's apple.

For the moment I simply stared blankly at him.

"But I have more treats in store for you before you die Cop," he told me.

"You would be better off killing me now Perry, because if I get my hands free for a moment I'm going to kill YOU!" I spat. *"This is inhuman!!!"*

Smiling, Perry stepped away from me and came back over with the cloth soaked in ether. He put me to sleep…again…

This time when I came to I was slumped over a table with my hands cuffed to the leg (of the table) under the table, my legs spread wide with some kind of bar on my ankles, and to make my situation even worse Perry had blindfolded me. My under shorts were off me at this point, and except for my shoes and socks I was balls ass naked.

"What the fuck are you going to do to me now you monster???" I roared like a caged animal.

"In prison the majority of the inmates made a big joke of my ass," Perry said. "They all used to take turns fucking me Officer Pig!!"

With that he gave my butt a real hard slap, causing me to yell out in pain. Perry stepped in front of me and yanked the blindfold off me. I saw on the table in front of me five dildos in assorted sizes, ranging from big to inhumanely gargantuan. He picked up the first one and rubbed the tip of it over my trembling lips.

"The inmates used to make sport of fucking my asshole Pig!!" he screamed in my face. "They all thought I had such an oh so sweet ass. At the end of a card game the winners would be the first ones to fuck my hole!! The bastards kept me tied down and waiting, just the way you are now! And now you will know what it feels like to have something so big pushed into your hole!! *You are going to know what it means to be raped, raped, and raped!!!*"

He had gone insane, completely over the edge. I hadn't seen it before, but I was helpless and in the clutches of a raving madman.

"P-Perry, don't do this!!" I said through my quivering lips.

He smiled mockingly and rapped me hard across the face with the dildo.

"Uhhhhhhrrrrr!!!" I yelled.

I saw that there was no reaching him. He was going to shove those dildos up my ass and there was nothing I could do to stop him. A wave of helplessness like I had never known washed over me.

"Let's begin," Perry said anxiously.

As Perry walked past me with the first dildo in his hand I noticed that my under shorts were tucked into his belt. Was he planning on keeping my Jockeys as a souvenir of all this? JEEZ! Perry stepped behind me and I felt his finger rubbing the tender flesh around my hole. He prodded it, sticking his finger in and quickly pulling it out.

Feeling beyond violated at that moment I roared, *"Perry, stop this!! Stop this now!!!"*

He ignored me…and continued teasing my hole with his finger. What he did next thoroughly disgusted me to say the least. He squatted down behind me, spread my ass cheeks apart and spit into my asshole a few times. Then, his finger was making squishing sounds against my hole. He prodded it again, sticking his finger in deeper this time. I clenched my teeth. When Perry pulled his finger out a loud fart escaped me. He laughed mockingly and held up the first dildo.

"You're ready…" he said breathlessly.

"Oh God no, no," I whimpered.

Perry began to push the dildo into my hole slowly, twisting it around at the same time. I screamed loud in agony and mortification. Just for the record I'm not gay and had never entertained the thought of someone fucking me in the ass. But after what Perry did to me I still wonder how those guys can take it. When the dildo was halfway in Perry gave it a hard push, ramming it home.

"AAARRRRGGGHHHH!!!!" I screamed.

My voice echoed and bounced off the walls of the big theater. I heard my echo everywhere. Perry gave my butt cheeks a few more hard slaps while the dildo was still inside me. He twisted it around, tormenting my insides.

"P-Perry, take it out!!!" I begged. *"My God!!!"*

"Are you that anxious for the second one?" Perry snickered.

He picked up the second dildo and held it up for me to see. I saw it through the welled up tears of pain in my eyes. It was bigger than the one that was now in my hole and a little fatter. I looked away from it with another scream of pain. Perry laughed and began pulling the first dildo slowly out of my hole. It came out painfully and my asshole made a popping sound when it was out. However, relief did not last long. Perry dropped the first dildo on the floor and began inserting the second one into my poor hole.

"ARRRRRRRR!!!!" I began screaming again.

In my agony I began pulling on the handcuffs on my wrists under the table leg, hoping to pull free and then kill the motherfucker! Sweat broke out all over me as the monster pushed the dildo into me. By now it was only halfway in and I felt as if my hole was being literally ripped apart.

"P-P-P-Perry...stop..." I begged.

But then, with a hard shove he rammed the dildo home, pushing it all the way in with one mean thrust. Suddenly the stage we were on seemed to be as bright as a sunny day at the beach. Everything was shiny and blurred in my vision. I heard the most unusual screeching noise and then realized it was coming from me... I was suffering pain like no other I had ever experienced. The thing inside me was being twisted around and my butt cheeks were being slapped hard over and over. I turned my head and looked at Perry.

"Perry, get that fucking thing out of me!!" I screamed.

"Fucking thing is the right word Pig, because that's just what it's doing to you, fucking," Perry said and smiled mockingly.

Then, he took my Jockey shorts out of his belt and stepped in front of me, leaving the dildo jammed in my hole.

"Your screaming and begging are beginning to bore me Romano Pig!!" Perry said. "I'm going to have to gag you."

With a quick flip he turned my under shorts inside out, revealing the skid-mark he'd teased me about earlier.

"Open wide," Perry said, waving the Jockeys in front of my face.

I had no choice but to do as I was told. I opened my mouth wide and Perry began pushing my under shorts into my craw, a section at a time. They tasted horrible. When I thought he couldn't possibly get them any further into my mouth Perry took a round metal instrument from his pocket and used it to cram the under shorts further in. I thought for sure he was going to choke me to death. My mouth was jammed up with white cotton, just a small piece of the elastic waistband protruding from between my lips.

"Tastes good eh?" Perry teased me, giving my puffed out face a hard slap.

"RRRRRmmmmffffff!!!" was the only reply I could make.

Perry pulled on the elastic sticking out from between my lips.

"Better make sure you stay gagged," he said.

He tied a rope over the Jockeys, jamming them securely into my mouth. The room spun in front of me. Perry returned to my backside and in a fast pull yanked the second dildo out of my hole. It came out followed by a loud smelly fart. Perry allowed me to relax for five minutes before he went to work on me with the third dildo. He held it up for me to see. It was bigger than the first two, longer, and fatter. Sweat poured off me and a look of disbelief mixed with terror filled my eyes. My asshole had been stretched to its limits by the first two dildos so this one was going to stretch me more.

"I'm going to turn your stinking butt-hole into a damned stinking pussy hole Cop," Perry said meanly.

Then, he spit twice into my rectal canal and wasted no goddamned time. I felt the third dildo being pushed in. When it was halfway in I thought I was going to pass out, but somehow I held on. Perry rapped my butt cheeks good and hard as he forced the third dildo into my hole. I screamed and sputtered through the gag in my mouth. Perry was merciless. He forced the thing all the way in. Tears flowed freely from my eyes. If this dildo was agony I wondered in outright terror what the fourth and fifth ones would be like. My asshole was on fire. It felt like I had been literally torn apart back there…my hole stretched to its limits. Perry was laughing mockingly and insanely.

"Like I told you Cop, in prison the other inmates made sport of fucking my asshole!" Perry yelled. "Now you know what I went through…and then some!"

He grabbed the dildo in my hole and twisted it around in there. Perry kept that third dildo in my rectum for a few more minutes and then he pulled it out. When this one came out I farted three times uncontrollably. I was being ruined back there, that was for sure. Perry ran his fingers over my stretched hole, teasing the tender flesh of it. Never in my life had I felt so utterly helpless. Perry then picked up the fourth dildo. It was <u>much </u>bigger than the third one. I struggled against the handcuffs and writhed up and down on the table.

"I haven't even put it inside you yet," Perry joked.

My legs were now numb from the damned ankle-bar he had on me and of course the handcuffs weren't going to give. I resigned myself to my impending fate. This time Perry was more merciless than the first three times. He didn't spit into my hole to lube me, (not that it helped anyhow) he didn't push the fourth dildo in slowly, and he wasted no time with it. He pressed the tip of it against my now very tender hole…and then pushed… And in one push the dildo was inside me. My vision blurred and I was definitely on the verge of passing out. I made small whimpering noises through my gag. From somewhere far away I heard insane laughter. I realized it was Perry as he slapped and slapped my butt cheeks. He fucked me with the fourth dildo…pulling it halfway out and then slamming it back inside me, over and over and over again. He continued laughing…

Finally, he pulled the dildo out of my hole. I didn't fart this time. Perry stepped in front of me with the ether soaked cloth in his hand.

"For the fifth and final dildo I have a very special treat for you," he said and pressed the cloth against my face.

The room went black.

When I woke up I found myself on top of the table on my back. The ankle-bar was still on me but my legs had been hoisted up and held there by a chain suspended from a ceiling rafter. The chain was connected to the ankle-bar. My hands were now cuffed behind me and my upper body was roped tight to the table. My under shorts were still crammed and tied into my mouth, gagging me. Perry was walking around the table with the fifth and most monstrous sized dildo of them all in his hand. I could not imagine how that thing was going to fit inside me. Perry saw that I had come to and leaned down, close to my pouting face.

"Your hole is really stretched good and fucking wide Cop," he said. "You even farted in your sleep."

Anger filled my eyes but all I could say to him was *"Mmmmmfffff!!!"* He patted my face, held up the fifth dildo and stepped to the end of the table. In the position I was now in my ass was in a very vulnerable spot. I felt Perry's fingers prodding my gaping hole. He spit into my rectum numerous times and kept prodding it till it was good and drenched. As his fingers went in and out I heard noises of slurping and squishing. I realized that the sounds were coming from my hole. Then, Perry announced that I was ready. He began pushing the fifth dildo into my sopping wet asshole. Sweat poured off me everywhere as the bastard forced that thing into my hole. When it was only halfway in my eyes rolled in my head and I screamed behind the gag. Unbelievably, a few minutes later the dildo was all the way in, torturing me in a way that I cannot describe. Perry laughed, cackled, and danced around the table I was trussed to. I looked at him through blurred vision…revenge on my mind… A few minutes later I was off the table and standing alone on the stage. My hands were still cuffed behind me, my jockeys were still in my mouth, the ankle-bar was off me, and the goddamned dildo was still wedged up in my hole, tormenting and torturing the fuck out of me. I had to hold my ass cheeks firmly in check so the device wouldn't slip out. You see, Perry was sitting in the first row of the audience section again and he had my gun in his hand, pointing it directly at me. He had told me that if the dildo slipped out of my hole he would shoot me. I was in a mortifying position, on stage, balls ass naked, with a damned dildo wedged up my ass. Perry played the part of my director, ordering me to walk back and forth on the stage. In order to stay alive I did as I was told. Perry laughed meanly at the sight of me walking and trying to keep the dildo in my hole at the same time. Next, he told me to stand on my tiptoes and turn myself in a clockwise direction. Once again I did as I was told. When Perry was done toying with me he came up on the stage, leaving my gun on the seat he'd just vacated. I looked longingly at that gun. Perry stood next to me and took me by my arm. Holding my arm in a firm grasp he grabbed the dildo with his other hand. He began thrusting it in and out of my hole, fucking me with it like crazy. My body lurched back and forth on the stage as I grunted in pain behind my gag. Then, all at once Perry yanked the dildo out of my hole and tossed it on the floor. The usual loud fart escaped from me. Perry untied the rope over my gag and pulled my Jockey shorts out of my mouth. A look of relief filled my eyes but it was short lived.

"We're far from done Cop!" Perry snapped.

He knelt down in front of me and put my under shorts back on me. I stepped into them like an obedient child.

"I have a special treat set up for you backstage!" my captor spat in my face. "Let's go!!"

I didn't say a word as Perry took my by my arm and led me off the stage. My asshole still felt like it was on fire and I was having trouble walking. Backstage, in a large dressing room I saw a massage-sized table set up with an oversized pot of boiling water next to it. Under the cauldron-like pot was a large Bunsen burner. In the oversized pot were mounds of beach-sized towels. The water looked as if it had been boiling for quite some time. Probably Perry had set it all up before he'd managed to capture me. I turned and looked angrily at my captor.

"What the hell is this all about?" I asked through clenched teeth. *"Haven't you done enough to me?!?"*

In a fast move Perry grabbed me and picked me up off the floor. He slammed me down on the table on my back and loomed over me.

"Done enough to you Pig?" Perry taunted me. "The torture is just getting started! You're going to be wishing I would just kill you and get it all the fuck over-with!!"

Then, he roped me tightly to the table in a criss-cross fashion. He gave my flat, washboard stomach a few hard slaps.

"We're ready," Perry announced.

With that said he pulled on a pair of rubber, elbow-length gloves. He reached into the over-sized cauldron-like pot and pulled out one of the steaming towels. It was smoking furiously.

"God no, Perry!!!" I screamed helplessly.

Ignoring me, Perry laid the towel over my body, covering me from my neck to my ankles.

"*Ohhhhhhhh...*" I moaned.

The hot steaming towel literally pulled the breath right out of me. I was struggling to breathe as Perry took a second towel out of the pot and laid it over the first one.

"*Ohhhhhhhhhh...*" I moaned again.

"People pay a lot for heat wraps in gyms and spas Cop!" Perry said. "You're getting it for free!"

He laid a third towel over me.

"Yeah, but the heat isn't this *fucking intense!!*" I managed to say.

He placed a fourth towel over my body.

"That's a bonus for you then cop, extra fucking HOT!" Perry laughed.

He placed a fifth towel over me and then tucked the ends under me. Steam was rising from the towels over me and by then I could hardly breathe.

"Now for the next layer," Perry said tauntingly.

I watched helplessly as Perry pulled a sixth towel out of the oversized cauldron-like pot. I passed out.

When I came to it was about three AM. I found myself back on the stage of the theater that Perry had me trapped in. I was back in my uniform but my hands were still cuffed behind me. I came to laying on the stage. Perry had the spotlight trained on me. Slowly, feeling pain in my asshole and the seared areas of my body where Perry had wrapped me in the hot towels I pulled myself slowly to my feet. I wondered how my body looked at this point. I mean, my nipples and balls had been electrified; my crotch and armpit hair had been shaved off, my asshole had been brutally, brutally molested by those dildos, and my body had been scorched by boiled towels. When I was finally standing I heard Perry's voice.

"Glad you're awake Officer Romano!" he said. "We are finally at the end of the production...the production being your life."

Because of the spotlight being the only light on I could not see Perry, but I guessed that he was sitting in his usual spot in the audience section of the theater, taunting me.

"Perry, if you're going to kill me then do it and get it over with, shoot me already!!" I ranted angrily.

Suddenly, the stage lights came back on and I saw that Perry was standing in the wings off the stage. He smiled and came over to me with my gun in his hand.

"Shoot you?" he asked, rubbing the gun against my face. "That would be too fast and easy. I have a better plan for you Pig!"

I looked at him head-on.

"What do you have in mind?" I asked him, trying to muster up some courage.

Perry pointed straight up to the balconies over the stage. We looked up together.

"As you can see this theater is quite high," Perry began. "You and I are going to take a walk up the steps to the highest balcony. A fall from there could kill a man."

My jaw dropped. Perry looked at me and smiled insanely.

"Would you care to lead the way Cop?" Perry asked, pointing my gun straight at my stomach.

"You actually expect me to walk to my death Perry?" I asked him defiantly.

He raised the gun to my head.

"If you would prefer to be shot to death right here I could do that," he replied. "You decide Cop."

I gulped hard, turned on my heel, and walked toward the stage steps leading to the balconies. Perry followed closely behind me.

"I knew you would make the right decision Pig," he snickered behind me.

I abruptly turned back to him and clenched my teeth in anger.

"You will be caught for this Perry!!" I spat.

With that I turned back to the steps and began climbing. As we climbed the steps Perry gave my ass a few slaps and pinches. He was planning to humiliate me till the end it seemed...or maybe the guy just liked my ass. About halfway up Perry ordered me to stop so he could catch his breath. He held my arm in a firm grasp. I looked down and saw how high up we already were. A few minutes went by and Perry waved the gun in my face.

"Mush!!" he ordered. "Move on!!"

I did as I was told, noticing that Perry was more winded than I was. Actually, he was a lot more winded than I was. I decided then and there that somehow or other I was going to get out of this alive. I would not let a lowlife like Perry Banks be my undoing. *But how???* My time was running out because we were almost to the top of the theater. Then I saw my answer. We were on the balcony just below the top one. I saw that there was a break in the guardrail. I slowed my pace, pretending to be getting winded. Perry snickered insanely behind me. When we got to the break in the guardrail I made my move. I turned quickly, took a few fast steps forward to put some distance between Perry and myself and kicked the gun out of Perry's hand.

"UFFFFF!!!" Perry sputtered in shock.

The gun flew out of his hand and down to the stage way below us. Before Perry could get his bearings I delivered another kick, this one to the guy's chest. Perry sputtered again, fell backward and landed against the guardrail.

"You son of a fucking bitch!!" he seethed, and without thinking charged at me.

I clenched my teeth and karate kicked him squarely in the stomach. I watched as Perry fell through the opening in the guardrail and to his death to the stage below. He went down screaming, landing in a bloody heap. I leaned against the wall dry heaving, crying, and gasping for breath for a few moments... not in pity for Perry's death, but for what he had done to me, and what he had almost succeeded in doing to me.

Slowly, although I was still in a lot of pain, I composed myself and walked back down the stairs to the stage. I found the key for the handcuffs on the seat Perry had sat on in the audience section of the theater. After releasing myself from the handcuffs I got my duty-belt, turned my dispatch radio back on, (Perry had turned it off right after capturing me.) and radioed for backup and an ambulance.

It took me three years to finally be able to tell that story. I've been to two therapists since that night trapped in a rundown theater, captured by Perry Banks. My body shows no telltale scars of that night, but the nightmares still persist and haunt me. In my dreams I can feel Perry pushing those dildos into my rectal hole and twisting them around inside me. Other times I dream of him electrifying my nipples and balls...and all the while he's laughing... laughing insanely at the poor trapped cop. I'm *still a cop, a damned good cop if I do say so myself.* I'm married now and my wife knows of the story. With the way I sometimes wake up screaming in the night from the nightmares there's no way she can't know. She is also trying to help me to put that night behind me. Maybe I will...someday.

THE STORY OF
JOHN AND DENNIS

My name is John Andrews. I'm writing this because I want to tell you about one of the hottest experiences I had recently. I'm about five feet ten inches tall; I have black short cut hair, a black neatly trimmed goatee, dark brown eyes, and muscles all over me from the constant workouts at the gym that I put myself through on a regular basis. I'm thirty-two years old and work as a systems analyst for a computer corporation in New York City. What I want to tell you about happened on a Saturday night not too long ago. Actually, because I still can't believe it happened, and that is actually why I am writing this. It had been a really rough week at work so on Saturday night I decided to treat myself to a few cold ones at the Local gay bar. Dressed all in black I sat at the bar sipping beer. When I was halfway through my second beer a blond, thin guy sat down on the stool next to me. I could feel him looking me over as he sat there. He looked to be about twenty-one or so and he was cute as a button. I don't usually go in for guys younger than I, but as I said, he was cute as a button. I looked at him and we smiled at each other. Not before too long I knew his name was Dennis and he knew my name was John. He bought me another beer and before long we were on our way back to my apartment. The little guy had made it more than clear that he loved worshipping the bodies of very muscular men. Well then, in that case I was his man...

When we got to my apartment we headed directly to the bedroom. In the bedroom Dennis dropped the backpack he was carrying on the floor and wasted no time. He threw his arms around my neck and kissed me hard on the lips, his tongue exploring my mouth like crazy. He sucked my tongue into his mouth and wrapped his lips around it, treating it like it was a dick. The guy sucked my tongue like crazy till it hurt. At one point I thought he was literally going to suck my tongue right out of my mouth. My knees turned to rubber as Dennis held me by my arms and kissed my face all over, kissed my neck, and planted soft delicate kisses over my eyes. His soft lips felt exquisite as he kissed my eyelids. He squeezed my biceps and covered my mouth with his again and again. He sucked my tongue, bit on my lips, and kissed me over and over again.

"Man oh man you are something else..." I said breathlessly as Dennis pulled my shirt off me and tossed it on the floor.

"Just let me take control big man..." Dennis said, his hands exploring my massive chest and big bouncy pecs. "You won't regret it, that I promise you..."

My dick was already rock hard in my jeans but when Dennis' mouth slurped onto one of my pink meaty nipples I went more than rock hard. I thought I would shoot my load right at that moment but I managed to control myself pretty well. Dennis ran his tongue over my nipples, sucking on them, biting on them, kissing them, and licking them. I ran my fingers through his silky blond hair as he drove me into a sexual frenzy. I was twice his fucking size but he was definitely taking control of me...and I wanted him to...*I really wanted him to!!* Dennis ran his hands over my broad shoulders, down over my chest, and back up again.

"Ohhhhhrrr yeahhhh..." I moaned loudly as he again slurped one of my nipples into his mouth.

When I crossed my hands up behind my head Dennis licked my armpits like crazy, sucking the sweat out of them. And let me tell you he was really making me sweat big fucking time. A little while later Dennis had me stripped naked and I was lying on my bed on my back. Dennis was stripped to his white briefs and kneeling on the side of me, licking my nipples like crazy and running his hands all over me, squeezing me, caressing me. The more than horny little fucker even knelt at the foot of my bed and tongue bathed my size eleven feet. He licked them all over, sucked on my toes, and chewed on the beefy bottoms of them. My fuckin' feet stink like crazy and this guy was licking and chewing on them like they smelled clean and fresh. My dick was hard and throbbing in between my legs, pointing straight up at the ceiling, begging for some attention, and begging for Dennis' hole... Oh yeah, more than anything I wanted to fuck him like crazy. Dennis stopped licking my feet and slowly crawled onto the bed over my legs and up to my crotch area. He straddled my well-toned thighs as I grabbed his hips and held him tight by them.

"Damn it you beautiful blond guy, you are driving me wild..." I said in a husky tone of voice.

I ran my hands over his briefs and snapped the elastic in them.

"I want to fuck you Beautiful guy..." I said breathlessly, caressing his hips. "I want to fuck you till I can't fuck you anymore..."

"Not yet..." Dennis said and reached down and squeezed my nipples hard.

I grimaced and looked up at him hungrily. He squeezed my nipples again.

"Yeah now, *I want to fuck you now...*" I said demandingly and pulled on Dennis' briefs.

"Let me do something else that will drive you more than wild big man..." Dennis said, looking at me lustfully.

"What do you have in mind?" I asked him.

"Let me tie you up." Dennis said and ran his fingers through my chest hair.

"What?" I asked him in a surprised tone of voice and sat up on my elbows. "Tie me up???"

"You'll love it, I promise..." Dennis said and placed his hands behind my neck.

I craned my head back and smiled at him.

"You're kidding, right Dennis?" I asked him.

"Not at all..." Dennis replied and caressed the back of my neck gently. "Nothing looks better than a big hunky guy like you all roped up good and tight..."

"I really don't get turned on by all that kinky shit..." I said and Dennis took his hands off the back of my neck.

He moved one finger lovingly over my goatee, trailing the outline of it. I kissed his finger when he touched it to my lips.

"Have you ever been all tied up during sex?" Dennis asked me.

"Honestly, no..." I said and he kissed me once on the lips.

He cradled my head in his hands and I kissed his nipples.

"So then if you've never tried it you don't know if you'll like it or not..." Dennis said and looked at me more hungrily than earlier.

"Come on you big fucking muscle guy, let me tie you the fuck up and really take control of you..." Dennis said breathlessly.

I took a deep breath and smiled at him. I decided to let the beautiful blond guy have his way, that's how fucking gorgeous he was.

"Okay Dennis, tie me up..." I said to him. "Then I fuck you, long and hard..."

Dennis smiled triumphantly, grabbed my wrists, and held them tightly together in front of me.

"All right!!!" he cried happily. "John, I am going to drive you insane!!"

Holding me by my wrists Dennis climbed off the bed, pulling me along with him. I played along, wanting the little guy to have his fun. He walked me across the room (my dick now painfully hard and throbbing in front of me and my balls hanging low filled to the max with my jizz) to where his backpack was on the floor.

"By the way, I don't have anything you can use to tie me up with..." I said as Dennis let go of my wrists.

He smiled, squatted down, and opened his backpack. He reached into the backpack and took out a length of white rope.

"I came prepared..." Dennis said with a big grin on his beautiful face.

I gulped hard, realizing that there was no getting out of it at that point. Dennis kneeled in front of me, grabbed me by my thighs, and ran his tongue over my bulging balls.

"Ohhhhrrr fuck..." I cried out in ecstasy. "Why'd I agree to let you tie me the fuck up???"

The way he was tongue bathing my balls made my dick even harder and made me want to fuck him even more...but I had to let him tie me up first...

Dennis sucked my balls, licked my balls, chewed on my balls, and slobbered over my balls till they felt like they were swollen to the size of tennis balls. He was making me wait to be tied up, making me wait to fuck him, and making me wait to cum. I was in a total heated frenzy when Dennis finally stopped tonguing my balls. They were slick with his saliva and real juicy looking now as they hung low between my legs. Droplets of pre cum oozed out of my piss hole and slid down the sides of my throbbing dick as Dennis stood up behind me, rope in hand. He pulled my hands behind my back and crossed them together at the wrists. My breath came in gasps as he slowly but tightly roped my hands behind me. When the little fucker was done tying my hands he took more rope out of the backpack and began tying my upper body, pinning my arms against my body. He tied rope around and around and around me, and I have to admit *it was turning me on*. There was something really strange and erotic about this guy who was a lot smaller than I overpowering me. My dick throbbed harder and harder like a thing totally alive. When Dennis was done tying my upper body I stood before him totally naked, bound, and at his mercy. He threw his arms around my neck and kissed my face as he ran his fingers through my hair.

"You have to do everything I say or I won't untie you." Dennis said with authority in his voice. "Is that clear?"

I could see he meant it so I quickly said "Yes Sir, its clear..."

"Good..." Dennis said and let go of me.

He squatted down and reached into another section of his backpack. He took out a pair of tit clamps and several metal ball bearings with long strings attached to them.

"Wh-what's all that for Dennis?" I asked him nervously.

"First rule, no questions or else I'll gag you." Dennis said to me. "You *have to* let me do whatever I want to you."

"O-okay Dennis..." I stammered, not too keen on the thought of being gagged.

He squeezed the tit clamps opened and slowly brought them toward my erect and pointy pink nipples.

"Dennis please..." I said as I felt the sharp teeth of the tit clamps against my nipples.

He closed the tit clamps onto my nipples and they bit into the tender flesh unmercifully.

"Arrrrhhh!!!" I yelled in pain.

Dennis smiled and took hold of the thin chain between the tit clamps. Using it as a leash he started walking me out of the bedroom.

"Wh-where are we goin' Dennis?" I asked him, sweat beginning to run over my muscular body.

"To your kitchen," Dennis replied, pulling me along by my aching nipples. "I noticed that you have a nice large round table in there..."

"What the hell does my kitchen table have to do with all this???" I asked, the pain in my nipples intensifying with each step I took.

Now, before I continue I want to make a few things clear here. I had never before allowed anyone, and I mean anyone to tie me up. Actually all the guys I met before Dennis didn't want to tie me up. Dennis somehow convinced me to allow him to do this to me. Also, I want to mention that even though I was in pain and helpless to stop the little fucker from abusing me I was totally turned on by it all. My damn dick didn't get soft once while he had me tightly trussed up. Okay, let me go on with the story now. Dennis walked me on my bare feet into my kitchen and over to the table. He left me standing next to the table and ran back to the bedroom. Great, I thought. I let the little fucker tie me up and now he's going to rob me. While I stood there totally helpless I looked down at myself. I was totally roped up and the muscles in my arms looked pretty magnificent under the binding ropes. My nipples looked pretty sorry though with those tit clamps on them.

"Errrhhh..." I said through clenched teeth as I strained mightily against the ropes.

Not a fucking chance of me getting myself untied. Dennis had tied me too fucking tight even to think about it. Big fucking muscle guy such as I am and I couldn't get myself untied. A few moments later Dennis came into the kitchen carrying his backpack in one hand and a pair of the metal ball bearings in his other hand. He put his backpack down on the floor and came over to me holding the ball bearings. He grabbed my arm and looked at me fiendishly.

"You ready to do as I tell you John?" Dennis asked me, squeezing my biceps.

"What do you have in mind for me Dennis?" I asked him, pain showing on my face. "Damn, my poor tits..."

"I want you to walk around your large kitchen table until I tell you to stop..." Dennis said to me.

"You've got to be kidding." I said, disbelief filling my eyes. "Is that it?"

"There's one other thing..." Dennis said, holding up the ball bearings.

"Oh shit..." I rasped as he squatted down in front of me.

I watched in agony as Dennis slowly tied the strings on the ball bearings around my balls. My balls, which were still throbbing and swollen from the tongue bathing that Dennis had given them earlier, were suddenly on fire with pain as he tied the long strings around them. When he finished he let go of the ball bearings and they plummeted to the floor, causing searing pain in my now bound nuts. The ball bearings were tied so they just reached the floor. I would be dragging them along with me as I walked around my kitchen table. My heart was thumping madly in my chest as my balls and nipples cried out in pain.

"Okay..." Dennis said, standing up next to me and grabbing my arm. "Time for you to take a walk...a long walk..."

"Dennis please..." I choked. "My balls man, my poor fucking balls..."

Dennis let go of my arm and slapped my ass hard.

"Get moving..." he said to me and stepped away from me.

I took a deep breath, let it out, and began walking slowly clockwise around the table. Each step was torture as I dragged the ball bearings with me by my aching balls.

"Arrrrhhh..." I moaned in agony and doubled over.

"Walk!!" Dennis commanded.

As I walked around the table Dennis took a leather riding crop out of his backpack. As I walked past him on the third revolution of the table he whacked my butt cheeks hard with the riding crop.

"Yowwww!!!" I roared and straightened up.

I looked at him in disbelief.

"Now hold on here Dennis..." I ranted. "Fuckin' tying me up is one thing and clamping my tits and torturing my balls is another but whacking me with that damned thing is out!!"

In response Dennis whacked me hard two more times on the ass with the riding crop. I yelped in pain.

"Move it John!!" he yelled at me and whacked me again with the riding crop. "Around the table!!"

I looked at him in defeat and slowly walked around the table.

"You're moving too slowly!!!" Dennis yelled and whacked my ass again.

"Ayyyyy!!!" I cried out in agony.

I tried to move faster to avoid being whacked with that damned riding crop but each step I took was an agony for my balls. And, no matter how fast I moved Dennis simply delighted in whacking my ass with that riding crop. After about fifteen times (I think) around the table Dennis ordered me to stop...and to stand at attention. With no choice but to obey I did as I was told. I was drenched in sweat and breathing unevenly as Dennis took the ball bearings off my balls.

"Ohhh thank you Dennis, thank you..." I said with relief. "And my balls thank you..."

He stood next to me and took the tit clamps off my nipples. However, he didn't make a single move to untie me yet.

"Do you have some ice water in the refrigerator?" Dennis asked me and squeezed one of my sore nipples. "You look like you could use some."

"Top shelf..." I gasped.

Dennis opened the refrigerator and took out a bottle of Poland Spring mineral water. He put it to my lips and I sipped it down.

"Ahhhh!!!" I sighed loudly. "Thank you Dennis..."

My dick was still hard and oozing pre cum as Dennis put the bottle of water back in the refrigerator. He gave my ass cheeks a tight squeeze and then took another pair of ball bearings from his backpack.

"Ready for another walk around your table John?" he asked me, holding up the ball bearings.

This pair was bigger and heavier looking than the first pair had been.

"Ohhhh no, no, no..." I said, choking back tears. "Dennis please..."

"Big muscle guy isn't so tough now eh?" Dennis teased me.

Slowly, and with a sinister look in his eyes Dennis squatted down in front of me. My balls were already hanging frightfully low from the first pair of ball bearings that Dennis had tied on them. I shuddered to think how they would look after the second pair had been on them. Dennis tied the strings on the ball bearings tightly around my aching nuts. As he did so I tried my best to remain standing at attention, grunting in pain. When Dennis was done he let go of the ball bearings. I screamed as they plummeted to the floor, tugging hard on my balls. Dennis smiled, grabbed my thighs, and ran his tongue over and over my tied and aching balls.

"Arrrrghhhh God no!!!" I cried, tears now streaming down my cheeks.

To comfort me just a little Dennis ran the tip of his tongue over the sides of my hard dick a few times. Then, he told me to get moving. I relaxed my stance of attention and took two small steps. It hurt ten times more than the first time to walk.

"Dennis...I can't..." I croaked. "It-it hurts too much man..."

I stood there shaking as he picked up the riding crop.

"Oh fuck no..." I croaked again and Dennis whacked my ass hard with the riding crop.

"Yowwchhh!!!" I screamed and began walking in tiny steps around the table.

My body shook and I heaved big breaths as I walked slowly around the table. Dennis didn't whack me too many times with the riding crop this time because he saw how much pain I was in already. I was sweating profusely at that point and my head was spinning. The ball bearings dragged along behind me as I walked and walked around my table...torturing me...

A little while later I doubled over as I walked and was breathing more than heavily. My balls felt like they would never be the same again. My dick however, remained amazingly hard. Finally Dennis told me to halt. I did as he said. When the ball bearings were off my nuts Dennis allowed me to sit down in a chair as he gave me water to drink.

"You're doing great big man..." Dennis said as I sipped the water.

"Thanks for the compliment..." I mumbled sarcastically.

He put the bottle of water away again and ordered me to stand up. I stood there helplessly as he reinforced all the ropes, making sure I could not get untied if I tried to.

"Dennis, I'm dying to fuck that hot ass of yours..." I whispered and kissed him on the top of his beautiful blond head.

Dennis looked at me, smiled, and kissed me on the lips.

"You'll just have to keep on waiting..." he mused and slapped my ass hard.

A few minutes later I was slumped over my kitchen table on my stomach, my feet dangling off the floor, and my legs spread wide, really wide, revealing my pink and puckered asshole. My hard dick and aching balls were pulled down behind my legs. Dennis was squatting behind me pouring peach flavored (edible) syrup all over my ass cheeks and into my asshole, making a treat for himself. When my ass cheeks and hole were thoroughly soaked with the sticky stuff Dennis stuck out his tongue and ran it over my ass cheeks and into my hole, gobbling up the peach syrup.

"Ohhhhrrr yeahhhh yeahhhh!!!" I roared, squirming real sexily on the table. "Fuckin' A Dennis!! That shit feels great!! Oh man, eat my hole Dennis you horny fucker!!!"

Dennis' tongue explored my hole like crazy, feasting on it, sucking on it, and practically devouring it. What I didn't know was that he was priming me for a big old butt plug. Dennis pursed his lips and pressed them against my now twitching bunghole. He slurped his lips against it, driving me further into a heated frenzy. My dick was throbbing like it was on fire behind my legs and I almost jumped off the table when Dennis ran his tongue over my aching balls. But then I saw the big butt plug that Dennis pulled out of his backpack...

Minutes later I was off the table and standing next to it with that monster of a butt plug in my hole. I squirmed miserably on my feet and stood at attention as Dennis tied a third set of ball bearings to my balls.

"Dennis no...no more ball bearings..." I pleaded miserably. "Fuck man, this butt plug is making me dizzy Dennis..."

My ass bucked back and forth as the butt plug tormented my hole. The third set of ball bearings was heavier and bigger than the first two sets had been. They made my balls feel like they were ten times their normal size. When they were securely tied onto my balls Dennis let go of them and I shrieked like mad when they hit the floor and dangled from my nuts. I looked at Dennis helplessly...

"Start walking." Dennis said sternly.

I looked at him in agony and my tears flowed freely.

"Dennis, I swear I can't..." I panted. "I can't fuckin' move..."

I stood there shaking as Dennis picked up the riding crop.

"All right, *all right!!!*" I ranted. "I'll fuckin' try man!!"

I took a couple of small steps and Dennis whacked me hard twice across the ass with the riding crop to get me moving faster. I yelped and plodded along, circling the table as best I could. I had made five slow revolutions when Dennis told me to stop. Sweating, I stood there as he clipped the tit clamps onto my nipples again. He told me to resume walking. I did as I was told.

"Fuckin' asshole I am to have gotten myself into this..." I muttered miserably.

After another ten revolutions around the table Dennis told me to stop. He came over to me and quickly untied the ball bearings from my balls. I heaved a sigh of relief as he then took the tit clamps off my nipples and yanked the butt plug out of my hole. My entire body was shaking and sweating as Dennis held me close, and stroked the hair on the back of my neck. I cried like a baby in his arms.

"You're okay John..." Dennis whispered in my ear and licked my earlobe. "You're really okay..."

He untied me completely and I sat down in a chair. My dick was still hard as a rock and waiting for Dennis' hole. He stepped in front of me and I placed my hands on his hips, hooking my thumbs into his underpants. I pulled him close to me and kissed his hairless chest.

"Are you mad at me?" he asked me.

"No, not at all." I replied and licked one of his nipples. "I agreed to let you have your way. I just hope you won't want to do that to me again next time."

"Next time???" Dennis asked me with a smile of joy on his face.

I slid his underpants down and off him.

"Yeah, next time Dennis..." I said and sat him down on my lap, my dick aimed at his hole.

Holding him by his hips I guided Dennis slowly onto my pole, entering him a little at a time. He squeezed my nipples as my dick nibbled hungrily at his hole.

"Ohhh yeahhh Dennis you are so fucking hot..." I whispered.

Slowly, he slid down onto my dick and began rocking up and down on it. I held him tightly by his hips as my dick plowed his hole.

"Ohhhh yeahhh John, fuck me..." Dennis crooned and ran his hands through my hair.

I happened to look down on the floor and saw the pile of rope that Dennis had used to tie me up with. Thinking about being roped up and at his mercy sent a shiver through me and I fucked him harder, hurting him erotically.

"Ohhhhhrrr God!!!" Dennis cried out.

"Fuckin' tied me up and tortured me you little fucker!!!" I seethed and fucked his hole more and more.

"Ohhhhrrr yeahhh yeah I did..." Dennis crooned breathlessly.

"I'm real glad I didn't lube your hole you little shit," I grunted as I thrust madly in and out of him. "I want you to really feel the deal of my cock..."

When I came I shot my hot load into Dennis' hole, filling it with my juices.

"Ohhhrrr yeahhhh yeah!!!" I roared thinking that people probably heard me way down the street.

As I shot my load I grabbed Dennis' hard dick and tugged it a few times. He came in gushes all over my chest, spewing his gobs and gobs of creamy spunk.

"Arrhhh yeahhh yeahhh..." he yelled as he shook like crazy on my dick.

When we were done Dennis slowly climbed off my dick and sat down on the floor at my feet. We looked at each other and smiled.

"Are your balls feeling okay?" he asked me and kissed them gently.

"Yeah, they're fine." I replied. "You worked 'em pretty hard but I'm a tough guy..."

"Yeah, you sure are..." Dennis said and kissed the top of each of my feet. "I'm exhausted."

"You're exhausted?" I asked him, a look of disbelief on my face. "After what you just put me through you're exhausted???"

Dennis smiled and said that torturing me had been hard work. I jumped to my feet, grabbed Dennis, and hoisted him over my shoulders and both of us laughing I carried him to my bedroom...

GREG ANDREWS AND
HIS BEER BUDDIES

My name is Greg Andrews; I'm a sales representative for a toy manufacturing company that is based in Ohio. My job entails that I travel a lot so each month or so I'm out in the field for a few days at a stretch. My wife doesn't mind as long as I keep my nose clean, if you know what I'm getting at. Although sometimes it sure is difficult for a guy to keep his nose clean, *if you know what I'm getting at.* I'm thirty years old. I stand six feet four inches tall I have black (corporate style cut) hair, crystal blue eyes and a smooth complexion. A clean, shavin' guy, that's me bud. What I want to tell you about herein happened pretty recently while I was on a business trip in New York City. I had just finished my meeting with the directors and chairmen of a big toy store.

"Well Mr. Andrews, it sure was a pleasure to meet you," Mr. Shaw, the chairman himself said to me as I stood packing my papers into my briefcase.

"Same here Mr. Shaw," I said, snapping my briefcase shut and turning to face him, he and I the last two guys in the boardroom where I'd just snagged one of the biggest accounts for my company.

"I can speak for the rest of the company reps when I say that we're very anxious to start doing business with you and your company," he said and with no hesitation twined his fingers around my tie and gave it a few pulls, toying with it as we spoke.

"Well, I can honestly say Sir that I feel the same way," I replied, feeling a slight chub in my suit pants as the old fart tugged at my tie. "I'm sure we'll all prosper very much from this deal."

He let go of my tie, we shook hands and I left the boardroom. Within ten minutes I was heading back to my hotel on the somewhat crowded afternoon train. I was handsomely dressed in a Giorgio Armani blue pinstriped suit, complete with black highly polished cap toe shoes. Sitting there looking over the papers from my meeting I couldn't help but notice the two men sitting across from me. They were looking at me pretty intently drinking me in was more like it, undressing me with their eyes. Jeez, first the chairman of the board makes a play for me tugging on my tie now these two check me out on the subway. This must be my lucky day I thought. As the two men continued to stare at me I finally recognized them when one of them smiled broadly at me. My heart raced and my mouth dropped open in shock.

"H-holy shit," I blurted happily, oblivious of everyone around us on the train. "Fuck, my two college buddies, Rick Cordero and David Taylor! I do not fucking believe it!"

"How's it hangin' Andrews?" Rick asked me, leaning forward in his seat.

"Hangin' as hung as ever you pervert," I replied with a grin.

I reached across, shook hands with both of them and moved to sit in between them.

"What the hell are you guys doing in New York?" I asked them. "And fuck man, what are the chances of me running into you like this after all this time?"

"We live here," David responded. "*And* we own a store here."

Rick held up a small suitcase and said that samples of what they sold at their store were in it. I lifted one of my big feet and rested it across my knee and congratulated them, adding that opening a business in New York and having it take off is no easy task. David placed his hand on my blue socked ankle and asked what I was doing in New York.

"I'm here on a business trip," I replied. "I'm staying at this real fucking ritzy hotel on Forty Ninth Street. Say, if you guys aren't busy why don't you come on up to my room? I have a full wet bar and we could catch up on some old times."

They looked at each other across me and said okay. David took his hand off my ankle and asked if I was married.

"Sure am," I said proudly. "Her name is Diane *and* she is beautiful."

"Any children?" Rick asked.

"No, not yet," I said. "I'm out in the field so damned much that we don't have the time just yet for children, know what I mean?"

"Yeah, we sure do," Rick said. "Work, work, work and more work."

"What about you two?" I asked them. "Are you guys married?"

"Not in the usual sense," David replied.

At that moment the train rolled into the forty-ninth street station. I collected my briefcase, David picked up their small suitcase and we all got off the train.

"Do you like New York?" Rick asked me as we walked toward the hotel through the crowded streets.

"Love it man," I replied happily. "I wish my wife and I could live here."

We got to the hotel; I checked the desk for messages (thankfully there were none) and all three of us walked to the elevator bank. We got on an elevator that was waiting and I pressed the number four.

"Real nice hotel," Rick said and took my upper arm in his hand. "But the least your company could do would be to provide you with a car and a driver to get you around. Riding the subway can be such a bitch. Not to mention that if the train gets stuck you could be late for important meetings."

"They do provide me with a car and a driver," I responded. "But I like the subway, most of the time it's quicker than riding around in traffic. And besides, if I hadn't been on the train I never would have run into you two."

"You do have a point there," David said.

The elevator stopped and the doors slid silently open. We stepped out onto the fourth floor. It was plush carpet, the walls were painted soft beige and the corridor was softly lit. Rick still held my upper arm as we walked toward my room. Being that we were old friends I didn't think anything of it. And based on the shit that he used to put me through in college I didn't think anything of it, more on that very soon.

"How long will you be in town for?" Rick asked me, squeezing my arm.

"Another two days and then I fly home to Ohio," I said.

When we reached my room Rick let go of my arm and I reached into my suit jacket pocket for my key. I opened the door and we all stepped inside. At that moment I had no clue as to what kind of afternoon it was going to turn out to be. I placed my briefcase on a table and walked over to the bar.

"Make yourselves comfortable guys," I said, reaching for some drinking glasses. "What can I get you?"

"Beer if you have it," Rick replied.

"Same for me," David said. "Brand isn't important, as long as it's cold."

I handed them each a Budweiser and mixed a vodka and orange juice for myself. Rick sat on a chair facing the couch that David and I had sat down on.

"So, how long have you been married?" Rick asked, starting a general conversation.

"Two and a half years," I replied and sipped my drink.

They each took a long gulp of their beers and I asked them what kind of business they owned. They were not wearing suits and ties so I guessed that it had to be a pretty casual sort of place they owned. They looked at each other and smiled wickedly before replying.

"You could say that we own a store that specializes in erotic merchandise," David responded. "Sort of like a pink Pussycat or The Pleasure Chest."

"Wow, you guys must do more than well then," I said and took a sip of my drink. "I hear that's a booming business these days, seeing as people are really exploring their more kinky sides."

"Sure is," Rick said and stood up.

He moved his chair to the center of the room and picked up their small suitcase.

"Would you perhaps care to sample some of our merchandise Greg?" Rick asked me with a glint in his eye.

"Sample what?" I asked him in reply, crossing a leg over my knee. "Just what do you guys have in mind?"

David squeezed my socked ankle and told me not to worry, adding that it would be fun, lots of fun, also saying that it would make my business trip all the more interesting.

"C'mon over here and sit down in this chair Tiger," Rick said to me encouragingly. "Do you remember when we used to call you Tiger back in college?"

"I remember," I said with a smile and stood up. "You guys called me Tiger because I was always on the prowl for some real fun."

I nervously adjusted the knot in my tie as I walked over to the chair Rick was standing next to. I sat down, arms at my sides. David then came over and stood next to Rick.

"Okay Tiger, face straight ahead and relax," Rick said and stroked the back of my hair a few times.

I heard the suitcase open and then in a flash and before I even knew what was happening each of them threw some rope over my upper body and pulled it tight around me. Before I had realized what the fuck was going on they were quickly winding rope over and over me in fast motions, tying me tightly to the chair.

"H-hey!!" I gasped in shock. "*Y-you two are tying me the fuck up!*"

"Relax Tiger," David said calmly. "You're getting a free demonstration here after all."

"Remember how I used to tie you up all the time in college Tiger?" Rick asked me teasingly.

"Yeah, every fucking chance you got," I replied sarcastically. "It was the first thing that crossed my mind when I saw you on the train earlier. And just like this you always managed to snag me by surprise every fucking time. Damn it David, I would be sitting there in my underpants and socks studying for an exam and the next thing I knew this fucking guy had me roped to my chair."

"And not just in his dorm room, nearly every time he came to my dorm room to study or to borrow a book I always managed to get this handsome dude all roped up," Rick said to David as they continued the task of binding me to the chair.

"Yeah, and one time he blindfolded me and had two girls come in and take turns sucking me off," I added. "Fucking bitches squeezed and sucked more loads out of me than I can even remember."

The two men looked at each other and snickered meanly. I suddenly had the feeling that it hadn't been two girls back in college that had repeatedly sucked me off that night in Rick's dorm room. Within a few short minutes my upper body was tightly roped to the chair, my suit jacket, shirt and tie wrinkled under the binding ropes.

"There," David said. "How does that feel?"

"Confining," I said to him, struggling in vain under the ropes.

"Say Tiger, do you have a basin or a really big bucket around here somewhere?" Rick asked me.

"In the bathroom under the sink," I said to him. "I use it to soak my feet in after I've done a lot of walking in the city. I asked the hotel management to have it sent up here. On my first night I was even lucky enough to have two bellboys come in and massage my feet in between soaking them."

"Lucky you," David said.

"Lucky them," Rick said with a smile and walked to the bathroom.

"Wait a minute here," I said to David. "What exactly does he have in mind? What the fuck have I gotten myself into here?"

I watched as David squatted at my feet and without a word slowly unlaced one of my cap toe shoes. Slowly, he pulled it off my foot and held my socked and smelly foot in his hand, caressing it, massaging it, and sending chills and thrills through me.

"Nice big executive feet you got Greg," David said to me, the smell from my socked foot wafting up at us. "No wonder Rick always tied you up every chance he got back in college."

He lifted my smelly, socked foot to his nose and sniffed it heartily. Then he licked the top and toes section of it a few times.

"Oh shit, *you fucking pervert,*" I gasped. "Look at you sniffing and licking my damned smelly foot."

Rick came out of the bathroom with the big white basin just as David was getting my other shoe off me. Rick stood by as David rolled my suit pants up at the bottom till they were over my calf length navy blue nylon dress socks. Then, David took the basin from Rick and placed it on the floor in front of my socked feet.

"Wh-what the hell are you guys going to do?" I asked them.

David lifted my feet and placed them in the basin, running his hands up and down my socks once my feet were in the basin. While David toyed with my socks Rick walked over to the bar and returned with several large-sized bottles of cold beer. I watched in awe as the two men then began opening the bottles and pouring the icy cold beer into the basin, soaking and submerging my socked feet with it.

"*Shit, that's fucking cold through my thin socks you guys,*" I rasped as the beer flowed over and over my socked feet.

I was in shock to also notice that my dick was chubbing up in my suit pants. In moments my socked feet were totally submerged in the beer, just to over my ankles. The two men smiled at each other.

"Feeling good Tiger?" Rick asked me and ran a hand through my hair, tousling it.

"Yeah, I suppose so," I replied, glancing down at my feet in the beer and wiggling my toes under my socks. "First time I've ever had my damned socks washed in beer though. When my wife and I do laundry we usually use Tide or Cheer."

We all laughed and then David told Rick to show me another piece of their erotic merchandise. Rick smiled wickedly, reached into the small suitcase and took out a leather hood with small eye, nose and mouth openings. I gulped hard as he slid it over my head and tied it slightly tight in the back.

"*Shit, shit, shit, of all the blasted things,*" I rasped again as the hood was tied on me.

"Damn, you were right David, a guy in a suit with a leather hood on his head sure makes a hot picture," Rick said.

The two men then knelt at my feet and they each lifted one of them out of the basin, beer dripping off my socks and into the basin. I watched through the eye slits in the hood as they squeezed my feet, getting some of the excess beer out of my socks. The smell of my stinky socks mixed with the cold beer wafted over us and my dick chubbed harder in my pants. Then, unbelievably to me, my two college buddies began sucking the beer out of my socks, stimulating me at the same time, and driving me wild.

"Ohhhhhh fuckers," I whispered. "Oh yeah, suck my feet, suck my socks, feels great."

They licked and slurped the tops of my big old feet and sucked my toes through my thin dress socks. My dick throbbed hard and mightily in my suit pants.

"Ohhhhhh yeah," I crooned. "Fucking foot freaks."

Holding one of my feet each they ran their tongues over and over my socks drooled on them and sucked up their saliva with the beer over and over. When my socks were pretty much drained of the beer they lowered my feet back into the basin again for another good beer soaking.

"Ohhhhhhh, *still so fucking cold,*" I whispered and wiggled my toes again under my socks.

"Tastes good huh?" Rick asked David.

"Sure does bud," David replied happily, holding one of my feet by the calf with one hand and trailing a finger over the submerged bottom of it at the same time, slightly tickling me. "Never sucked beer off a pair of executive socked feet before. I really prefer drinking beer this way to a mug or glass any fucking day."

"Yeah, next time we're in a bar and the bartender asks if we want a mug with our beer we should tell him no, put it on that suit guy's socks over there," Rick said and the two men laughed.

Again they each held one of my big smelly socked feet aloft and sucked and licked them all over, sucking and drinking up the beer and foot sweat that was pouring through my socks.

"Oh God, this shit *is* driving me fucking wild," I said to them. "Fucking best business trip I've ever been on."

"What would your wife say?" Rick asked me teasingly and sucked one of my socked toes like crazy, sending chills through me.

"My wife never sucked my damned feet," I responded. "She won't say anything."

For the next few minutes the two men didn't say a word. The only sounds in the room for those few minutes were the sounds of them slurping up the beer from my sopped socks. They again and again ran their tongues up and down and all over my socks, flicking over my ankles and calves, driving me into utter ecstasy. My dick was pounding long and hard in my suit pants, begging for release. I could feel the pre cum oozing from my wide piss slit.

"Ohhh yeah, yeah," I whispered breathlessly.

When the beer was gone from my socks a second time the two men amused themselves massaging my big feet and then looked at each other.

"There really is something about a handsome guy's smelly dress socked feet huh?" David asked Rick, holding one of my feet close to his nose and mouth.

"Yeah, I'll definitely agree with that," Rick replied, holding my other foot equally as close to his nose and mouth.

"One more time Rick," David said pleadingly. "His fucking socks taste and stink like magic with the beer on them."

Rick shrugged as if I didn't have a word to say in the matter and they submerged my socked feet in the basin a third time.

"Oooooo yeah," I murmured as my socks absorbed the beer.

Rick and David went crazy a third time sucking and licking the beer out of my socks, teasing my toes with the tips of their tongues. This time when the beer was all sucked out of my socks they didn't stop working my feet. They pulled my socks off my feet and began working my bare very smelly feet. They sucked each of my toes as if it were a dick, sniffed in between my toes like crazy and licked in there also. Needless to say I was now more than pounding a hard-on in my suit pants. They bathed the tops and bottoms of my feet with their tongues; tongue bathed my ankles and calves and moved back to my toes till I thought I would go more than totally ape shit. Actually, I would go more than ape shit. I was totally alive with goose bumps all over me and my dick was more than pounding like a thing alive in my pants. Never in my life did I ever think that I could become so aroused by having two of my buddies service my feet for me.

"Fuck, I want to shoot a load so fucking bad you guys," I said breathlessly. "Please, *please,* I never knew I could get off like this. Fuck man, I'll even cream my load right in my damned underwear. Now I know why you two tied me the fuck up."

The two men stopped working my feet, dropped them to the sides of the chair and quickly untied me. I pulled the leather hood off and yanked my crank out of the fly opening of my suit pants. As I slowly stroked myself Rick and David resumed servicing my bare feet.

"Ohhh yeah, lick my damned smelly feet you two," I moaned as I jacked off.

When I came I caught my goop in my hands, smeared it over my feet and Rick and David hastily licked it off, sending more goose bumps and chills through me. They sucked my cum off my toes and swirled their tongues over and over the bottoms of my feet. I sat there looking at them with a smile of satisfaction on my face. When they were done they looked up at me. We all smiled real big at each other.

"So, this is the kind of business you guys are in," I mused.

"Sure is Greg," Rick responded and squeezed one of my bare feet. "The merchandise we sell allows and helps people to explore their kinky sexual fantasies."

I sat back in thought for a good minute or so.

"Say, I have an idea," I said, looking at the beer still in the basin. "I really don't want all that beer going to waste."

"What do you have in mind Tiger?" Rick asked me, as if he didn't know already.

"David, go in the bathroom," I said. "There's a hamper in there filled with dirty clothes. This hotel provides laundry service for execs like me. In the hamper you'll find my black nylon dress socks from yesterday. Shit man, being in that hamper must surely have scented them up real nice and ripe."

Smiling, David dashed anxiously to the bathroom.

"You know the rules buddy," Rick said, holding up the rope and leering lustfully at me...

Moments later my black nylon dress socks from the day before were on my feet and fuck man, *they smelled more than ripe.* I was again tied to my chair as Rick submerged my smelly-socked feet in the beer.

"Fucking blast number two coming up," I said softly as the two men began slurping at my feet again.

That, I must admit was the best and most interesting business trip I was ever sent on. Now, when my company has business in New York City I always look forward to getting my tired and smelly executive feet serviced by my two kinky buddies who live there. I sure am glad that fate brought us all back together...

RALPH

"Ohhhhrrr, Shit, shit!!!!" I grunted angrily and miserably as I desperately tried to get myself untied from the straight backed chair I was sitting on. *"Fuckers*!!! Some work buddies they turned out to be!!! A joke they had said, just for fun they had said. Come on Ralph, you'll love it they had claimed!! *Fucking idiot I am!!!* Can't believe I went along with that stupid and fucked up game!!!"

I was trapped in a hotel room in New York City. I was wearing just my white Calvin Klein boxer shorts, (the tip of my semi hard pecker sticking out of the fly opening in them, oozing droplets of pre cum) a pair of calf length black ribbed nylon dress socks, and burgundy colored lace-up dress shoes while my two work associates David and Alex were attending the meeting *we* had all gone there for.

"UUUUhhhhrrrr shit!!!" I ranted angrily as I struggled helplessly under the tight and binding ropes. "Got to get myself untied and to that damned meeting!! *I'm* the account executive after all!!!"

I was tied very securely to the chair, not really a chance of getting untied whatsoever…but I had to try man, shit, *I had to fucking try*. Mounds of rope were wound around and around my muscular upper body, pinning me to the chair. My hands were trapped behind me, tied together and roped off to the back rung of the chair. My thighs were tied down to the chair, preventing me from standing up, and my socked ankles were each tied to the legs of the chair. What a fucked up position for a bank executive to be in I thought miserably. I continued struggling to get myself untied... Alas, as I struggled I heard a key slide into the lock of the hotel room door. I silently prayed that it was Alex and David, finally returning to untie me. Instead two bellboys walked into the room, looking at me hungrily.

"Awwwhhh no no, not again with this shit..." I muttered angrily, watching as the two faggot bellboys locked the door.

"Good afternoon Ralph..." the blond guy said to me as he and his dark haired buddy walked over to me.

"Look, could we skip this shit please and just get to the part where you guys may untie me?" I asked them sarcastically. "I mean, two of your perverted buddies were here not too long ago!!"

I glanced down at my chest and saw the remnants of the cum that had dried up and some that was still drying up all over my somewhat hairy chest, the reminder that two bellboys had been here earlier... My nipples looked awful, seeing as they had been sucked and tortured like crazy by four guys already...and I had the distinct feeling that these two guys were going to have their way with my nips as well...

The two bellboys squatted at my sides, ran their hands over my chest, squeezed my nipples, and twisted them and pinched them.

"Ahhhrrr shit..." I groaned. "Fuckin' Alex and David will pay for this shit..."

As the two bellboys toyed with my chest and nipples my pecker grew hard in my under shorts. The dark haired bellboy took it by the tip and slid it out of the fly opening of my Calvin Klein's, pinching the tip of it real hard, along with my big hairy balls.

"Ohhhhrrr no no…" I grunted miserably and helplessly. "Leave my dick alone you guys…fuckin' guy is so sore already…"

"We have to shut this executive guy up…" the blond bellboy said irritably.

He stood up, walked over to my opened luggage, and picked up a pair of my knee length black dress socks.

"Hey man, leave my socks alone!!" I demanded harshly. The first sock he rolled up into a ball, crammed it in my mouth, and tied the other sock over it, jamming it tightly in my mouth. When I had packed my luggage for this business trip I never once imagined a pair of my dress socks being crammed in my mouth as a gag. The only consolation I had was that it was a fresh pair of socks he had crammed into my mouth and not a used pair, like for instance, the ones I was wearing…*god of gods that would have been awful!!* My wife refuses to handle my socks at the end of the day because they stink so badly when I take them off. She demands that I put them directly into the washing machine myself…

"RRRRmmmmfffff!!!" I sputtered angrily as the two bellboys proceeded to slurp one of my sore nipples each into their greedy mouths. As I sat there feeling totally helpless and being feasted upon like a damned buffet I thought back on how I had come to wind up in this damned position…

My name is Ralph and I work for a Chicago based bank as an account executive. I'm five feet ten inches tall, I have dark brown hair, (cut in a banker's cut) deep brown eyes, and my body is muscular and much chiseled from working out regularly at the gym. I'm twenty eight years old, one of the youngest account executives to ever work for the bank I work for… and damned proud of it if I do say so myself. I'm married (for the last three years) to a beautiful woman named Laura. Because I am the account executive for a toy manufacturing company that is based in New York City it is part of my job to attend the monthly meetings that are held there. On this particular trip David and Alex came along with me…to learn the ropes so to speak. (Little did I know that it would be me learning the ropes…literally…) They are both junior executives with the bank, and my senior manager, Mr. Franklin thought it would be a good idea for them to accompany me on this trip. I had no choice but to agree. So, on Monday morning David, Alex, and I arrived in our hotel room in New York City for our four-day trip, all of us clad in dark colored suits and silk ties. We tipped the bellboys (two of which came to the room later on and had their way with me) who had carried our luggage to our room and settled down. I sat down behind the desk that was in the large room and propped my feet up on it.

"Well guys, here we are..." I said with a grin. "Welcome to the lap of luxury..."

"There are only two queen sized beds..." Alex said, looking at me quizzically. "Two of us will have to share a bed."

"Fuck that!" I said, crossing my big feet at the ankles on the desk. "You two clowns can sleep together. I'm a married man after all..."

We all laughed loudly at my remark.

"How long till we have to be at the first meeting?" Alex asked me, walking over to me and sitting on the desk, right next to my propped up feet.

"We still have a couple of hours..." I replied, looking at my watch. "We can relax for a while before going over the paperwork and what we'll be discussing at the meeting."

"How about a game of cards before we get down to business Boss man?" Alex asked me, placing a hand around one of my black socked ankles and squeezing it.

"Cards?" I asked him as he held tightly to my foot. "You want to play cards?"

"Yeah, that sounds like a good idea..." David chimed in from across the room. "It'll relax us before the meeting..."

"I'm already relaxed." I said, crossing my hands behind my neck, not really paying attention to the fact that Alex still had his hand on my foot. "I've done this sort of thing many times before...I'm not worried about a thing."

"Well maybe we are." Alex said and snapped my sock against my ankle. "Come on Boss man, one game of cards..."

Why I didn't tell that guy to get his paw off my ankle and leave my sock alone I don't know.

"Yeah, and just to sweeten things up we can really make the game interesting." David said from across the room.

"You mean play for money?" I asked him, not turning around.

"No, the guy who loses the game has to strip to his underpants and shoes and socks and allow the other two guys to rope him to a chair." David said fiendishly.

"What??? " I guffawed; pulling my feet off the desk, and turning around to look at David as he sat there on the bed grinning from ear to ear. "Are you out of your fucking mind? Strip a guy and rope him to a chair? What in hell kind of fucked up shit is that???"

"Sure, it's a game my friends and I used to play when we were teenagers." David said.

"And how did you fare at it when you were a teenager?" I asked him sarcastically.

"Well, let's say I spent a lot of time tied up..."David replied and we all broke out in laughter.

"I'm game for it." Alex piped up anxiously. "Come on Boss man, let's do it. It'll be fun. And when David loses we can tie him the fuck up in his drawers and shoes and socks."

"I don't have a deck of cards," I said.

"I do," Alex said, walking over to his luggage and opening it.

"I also don't have any rope..." I added sheepishly, wondering if this was a good idea.

"I have that...," David said slyly, opening his luggage.

"You brought rope with you on a business trip?" I asked David, a look of disbelief on my face.

"Sure, you never know when you're going to be playing a game of cards," David responded with a wicked looking grin on his face.

Hell of a way to play cards I thought.

"I don't know about this guys...," I said, sounding slightly uncertain.

"Come on Boss man, it'll be fun, just a game, and a good joke at the end of the game for the loser..." David said insistently.

"Okay, but after we're done we have to get to that meeting..." I said sternly. "Deal?"

"Deal." the two men said in unison.

We all stood up, shucked off our suit coats, tossed them on a bed, and loosened our ties.

"What game should we play?" I asked as we all sat down around the writing table.

"Something old and easy..." Alex said. "Let's play Go fish...the guy who loses all his cards first is the loser."

"Sounds good to me," David said. "And may I add that I can't wait to find out what kind of underwear you wear Boss man..."

At that we all laughed and I, being the boss man, began dealing the cards.

Well, it didn't take long to see that I was losing the game miserably. Within the first three rounds I had lost just about every call. When the game was halfway over and it looked like Alex was in the lead my heart started pounding nervously in my chest.

"Say uh, Alex, you got any king cards?" I asked, tugging on my tie and starting to sweat.

"Nah..." Alex replied and looked fiendishly at David

I gulped, because I knew at that moment that David had three king cards... and I didn't need three guesses to know what he was going to ask me.

"Okay Boss man, you got any king cards?" David asked me, and he and Alex laughed hysterically.

With a look of total defeat on my face I handed over my king card. I knew that I didn't have to go along with the rules we had set up for at the end of the game...but I also knew that if I came out a winner I would gladly go along with the rules. I decided to be a good sport and stick it out. I mean, okay, so I would have to strip to my shoes, socks, and under shorts. No fucking big deal really. I mean, I had been in the locker room at the gym countless times. I had been naked in front of total strangers. Here, I would still be wearing my underpants and shoes and socks. No big deal because I knew David and Alex. Then, *shit*, then David and Alex would tie me up for a while. Just for a short while...and then we would go to the meeting. Wasn't that right? Yeah, right.

I was down to two lousy cards, not a chance of even making a comeback in the game at some point. I nervously tugged on my tie, asked Alex if he had any tens, and he simply shook his head "no." Obviously David was holding the ten cards. David snickered and asked me if I had any tens. I handed over the card, holding my one card left in my hand. I pulled miserably on my tie.

"You know Boss man, if I were you I would just take that tie off my neck now..." Alex said with a leer. "...because it'll be coming off you soon anyhow..."

"It ain't over till it's over..." I whispered, gripping my last card tightly in my fingers.

"Well it will be over now..." David piped up, a mocking grin on his face. "Tell me boss man, by any chance, are you holding a four of clubs there?"

I tossed my last card over to David, a look of utter defeat all over my face. The two men laughed mockingly, gave each other a loud high five, and stood up. From the way they were acting it seemed like they had actually been hoping I would lose the game.

"Okay boss man; let's see what style of underpants you wear..." David crowed wickedly.

I pulled myself to my feet, whispered the word *"shit"* three times and undid the knot in my tie. As I stood there unbuttoning my white dress shirt Alex placed a straight-back chair in the center of the room.

"Your throne Boss man..." Alex snickered.

"Shit..." I muttered. "You two are really going to tie me the fuck up?"

"Sure as shit." Alex quipped merrily. "You agreed to the rules after all. Now hurry up and strip. We have a meeting to get to after all."

"Shit man, horrible way to treat the boss," I said with a mock grin on my face.

I angrily pulled my shirttails out of my suit pants and shucked the shirt off, tossing it onto the bed along with my tie and suit jacket. I stood there with my big muscular chest bared as I undid my belt and the button on my suit pants. Alex and David were standing by the chair, each of them holding a good amount of rope in their hands. I actually got the feeling they were looking at me lustfully as I slid my pants off myself over my shoes and socks. I tossed my pants onto the bed along with my other discarded clothing and stood there in just my white Calvin Klein boxer shorts, my calf length black nylon ribbed dress socks, and my burgundy colored lace-up dress shoes.

"Boxers David, I wear boxer shorts..." I said to David as I stood there feeling really stupid and totally vulnerable. "My wife thinks they look real good on me..."

The two men gestured with their index fingers for me to come over to them and sit down.

"Come on boss man, time for you to fulfill the rest of the rules of the game." Alex said to me. "Come and get tied up."

I took a deep, defeated sounding breath, walked over to the chair, and sat down. If I didn't know better I would have sworn that my pecker was getting slightly hard in my under shorts.

"Hands behind you Boss man, and press them against the back rung of the chair." David instructed me as they squatted at my sides.

I did as I was told and the two men quickly went to work binding me to the chair.

"Er, how long will you leave me tied up for?" I asked them. "I never asked that earlier…how long a guy has to stay tied up…"

"Not too long Boss man…" David replied as he pulled a good length of rope around my upper body, pinning me to the chair. "Just until *you* manage to get yourself untied."

"What?" I asked them, sounding somewhat nervous, but still trying to remain cool.

"Yeah, that's the rule." David replied. "The guy who gets tied up has to stay tied up until *he* manages to free himself."

Once my hands and upper body were tightly roped to the chair the two men pressed my feet against the legs of the chair and began tying them to the legs of the chair.

"B-but you're tying me so fucking tight…" I said, my lips beginning to tremble, and also realizing too late that I had made a serious and stupid mistake.

"Well, if we tied you loosely it wouldn't be any fun watching you struggle now would it?" Alex asked me tauntingly and snapped the elastic in my sock against my leg.

"No, I guess not…" I said sheepishly and they finished tying my feet.

Moments later they were standing over me, looking me over with satisfaction showing on their faces.

"Think you'll get untied before that meeting starts Boss man?" Alex asked me.

"Hey now, hold on there," I said, starting to struggle to get free at that moment. "If I don't get myself untied in ample time for that meeting you two jokers had *better* fucking untie me!!"

"Sorry Boss man, but the rules still apply..." Alex said, reached down, and gave one of my nipples a hard squeeze.

"OUCH!!" I gasped. "Leave my tits alone you pervert!!"

"He struggles real nicely, don't you think?" Alex asked David and gave my nipple another hard squeeze, followed by twisting it real painfully.

"Uhhhrrr..." I roared angrily. "Your rules didn't say anything about hurting the boss man's nips..."

The two men squatted at my sides and looked hungrily and longingly at my silver dollar sized, erect, brown nipples. Actually, their tongues were just about hanging out of their mouths as they looked at my damned nipples.

"You know David, his tits look as good and delicious as a woman's." Alex commented, placing his thumb and first two fingers tightly around one of my nipples. "They look sort of like the tits this girl I dated a while back had."

"Really now?" David asked jokingly, hooking his thumb and first two fingers around my other nipple, clamping his fingers down on it.

The two men squeezed, twisted, and pulled hard on my poor nips.

"Uhhhhnnnfff shit!!!" I roared angrily.

"Yeah, really," Alex went on. "She loved when I played with those nips of hers, but most of all, most of all man, she *really fucking* loved when I would tongue, bite, and slurp the fuck outa those tits for her."

Alex and David looked tauntingly into my eyes.

"Y-you wouldn't..." I muttered as they squeezed my nipples harder and harder. "You fucking guys, you wouldn't... I mean, I'm a married man after all..."

"Married or not Boss man, you can still have your nips tortured." Alex quipped, took his fingers off my nipple, and clamped his mouth down on it.

"Arrrhhh shit..." I gasped as Alex slurped his lips, teeth, and tongue onto my nipple.

I looked down at David as he took his fingers off my other nipple.

"No man, come on, don't..." I pleaded.

"Just get yourself untied Boss man and then we'll stop..." David said and clamped his mouth down hard on my other nipple.

"Arrrghhh GOD..." I grunted angrily as the two men really slurped the fuck out of my nips, making loud squishing sounds as they really went to town on them.

"Can't believe this shit!!" I grunted angrily and miserably. "You two perverts are fucking eating my tits for lunch!!"

They drooled like mad onto my nipples, quickly sucking up their saliva, hurting and tormenting my poor nips at the same time.

"Ohhhhh shit you guys..." I gasped, trying desperately to get myself untied.

As they sucked and slurped my nipples harder and harder my pecker was suddenly real hard and the tip of it was sticking out of the fly opening in my boxer shorts. The two men hadn't noticed it yet though. They were still too busy eating my nips.

"Damn you guys, my wife doesn't eat my tits like you two are doing right now..." I said breathlessly. "Actually, she doesn't eat my nips at all..."

As the two men went on really working the fuck out of my nips I tried desperately to get untied. They ran their hands over my thighs, down my legs, and toyed with my black dress socks. My dick grew harder, the tip of it peeking out of the fly opening in my boxer shorts.

"Arrrhhhh…" I gasped, looking down at the two men as they ate my tits more and more. "C-come on you jokers, enough of this already!! You've had your fun. I lost the game, you got me to strip for you, you fucking tied me up…"

At that point I clenched my teeth in agony because Alex and David had clamped their front teeth down on the tips of my nipples. They yanked the tips of my nipples real hard with their front teeth.

"Ayyyyyrrr shit…and you fuckers, you got to eat the boss man's nips for lunch!!" I squealed through my clenched teeth, watching in tortured agony as the two men really bit down on my poor nips. "Now fucking untie me already!! Ohhhhrrr GOD, I don't believe this shit!!"

Just when I thought they were going to literally bite my nips clear off my chest they stopped biting them, and quickly slurped their lips around them again. They resumed sucking, slurping, and licking at my nips like crazy, beginning to make me dizzy. When my nips were more than erect and pointy on my chest they stopped sucking, slurping, and licking them, only to take them between their front teeth again and bite the fuck out of them all over again.

"Arrrhhhhh…know what you two are?" I asked them angrily. "Faggots, tit loving faggots!! That's what you two perverts are!! Fuck it all, I wound up on a business trip and got roped up by two damned faggots!!"

Their hands moved up and down my legs as they went on and on torturing the fuck out of my poor nipples. They snapped my socks against my calves, tugged on my shoelaces, and squeezed my thighs real hard. I began sweating like crazy.

"Guys please…" I moaned with my head tilted back, looking up at the ceiling, sweat rolling off me like crazy now.

"Can't believe we're fucking chowing down on the boss man's tits..." Alex said merrily, taking his mouth off my nipple for a moment.

"You can't believe it?" David asked in reply. "Shit man, I've only been thinking about doing something like this to him for the longest fucking time."

As they spoke to each other they used their fingers and thumbs on my nipples, pinching, squeezing, pulling, twisting, and tweaking my poor nips. That way my nips would have no let-up on being tortured.

"Glad you came up with that idea for the loser of the card game..." Alex said as he gave my nipple between his fingers a tight squeeze.

"Ooouuucchhh jeez..." I gasped.

"Yeah, me too, but it's my childhood friends you should really thank." David said. "They were the ones who came up with that shit years ago."

The way they were talking about me as if I wasn't even there was really pissing me off, infuriating me to say the least. The way they were putting the screws to my poor nips was more than infuriating me though; it was driving me fucking crazy, in more ways than one...

When they were done talking they clamped their mouths back down on my nips *again*. The way they sucked at them this time it felt like two electronic suction cups had been attached to my poor nips.

"Arrrrrhhh GOD, stop this shit already!!" I grunted miserably.

As they sucked, slurped, bit, and even planted small delicate kisses on my nipples my dick stood up outside the fly opening of my under shorts, betraying the fuck out of me.

"Well well, well, would you look at that?" Alex asked me tauntingly as droplets upon droplets of pre cum oozed out of my dick slit and slid down the sides of it. "Fuckin' boss man is enjoying having us eat his tits."

David abandoned my other nipple and looked down at my hard dick also.

"Shit man, you're right." David said, looking hungrily at my hard dick. "That boner is telling a story…"

"Once upon a time there was a handsome account executive named Ralph who was stupid enough to get himself trapped into a really sick position…" Alex snickered, wrapping a fist tightly around the shaft of my throbbing dick. "And two junior executives named Alex and David who wound up having Ralph's tits for lunch."

"Ohhhrrr fuck, no no…" I panted breathlessly as Alex held my throbbing dick tightly in his fist.

Alex began slowly stroking my dick.

"Ohhhrr no no, not this man…" I pleaded.

"Goin' to get him off eh?" David asked Alex.

"A few good strokes ought to do it man." Alex said, looking at my dick in awe in his hand. "Man oh man, his meat is actually all warm and twitching in my hand David. Want to feel it?"

"Don't mind if I do." David replied.

Alex let go of my dick and David quickly took it in his fist, stroking it.

"Oh yeah, you're right man, fuckin' well-done tube steak this executive guy has…" David said, leering up at me, stroking me faster and faster.

"Ohhh no no, I'm getting' close you perverts…" I seethed. "Fuckers are going to make me shoot my damned load."

And then, sure enough, as David stroked me faster and faster I shot a hefty sized load of executive jizz all over my chest and nipples, dripping down onto my stomach area.

"Ohhhrrr shit, yeah yeah!!!" I grunted loudly, squirming under the ropes in a mixture of anger and ecstasy. *"Fuckers*, makin' me shoot my damned load…"

"Say Boss man, when was the last time your wife gave you some good sex?" Alex asked me as David went on stroking me, getting more and more jizz out of me. "What a king sized load. You must really have enjoyed having us eat those nips of yours…"

Actually, it did seem to go on and on as David pumped my dick like crazy. Ropes upon ropes of thick juicy sperm were erupting like crazy from my dick slit.

"Uhhhhnnn…" I gasped breathlessly.

When I was finally done David let go of my dick and my chest, nipples, and stomach areas were a mess with my thick creamy cum. It soaked the ropes over my chest area and dripped down to my stomach. My semi hard dick lay in my under shorts. It was peeking out of the fly opening like a dog that had been caught doing something it shouldn't be doing.

"Man, look at that." David said. "Fuckin' executive boy just cooked desert for us…"

"Oh no no, you guys wouldn't…" I said in utter disbelief.

But alas, to my dismay they did. They stuck out their big tongues and began lapping my cum off me.

"Ohhhrrr no no…*damned faggots!!!*" I seethed, curling my socked toes back in my shoes as chills coursed all through me. "Lickin' me like I was an ice cream cone!!"

When just about all of my cum had been licked off my chest and stomach areas the two tit hungry junior executives *again* clamped their mouths down on my overly sore nipples.

"Arrrghhhh shit!!" I ranted as chills swept through me.

I had found that after shooting my load my nipples became super sensitive to the touch. Having these two guys (or anybody for that matter) slurp at them at that moment was the last thing I wanted. But alas, at the moment what I wanted was not up to me whatsoever.

After another fifteen or twenty minutes or so of really eating my tits all over again they finally stopped and stood up.

"Ohhh man thanks you guys…" I panted. "Didn't think I could take much more of that shit. Untie me now and I'll forget about all of this."

"Think we better head to that meeting?" David asked Alex, looking at his watch. "We don't want to be late after all."

"Yeah, that's a good idea." Alex said, tightening his tie at his neck. "And if anyone there asks for the boss man here we'll just say he got a little tied up and couldn't make the first meeting."

"Hey now wait a minute." I said worriedly. "I *have* to be at that meeting!! I am the goddamned account executive! Fucking untie me now you sick fucks!!"

I struggled like crazy as they pulled on their suit jackets and collected legal pads and pens from their luggage.

"Guys come on!!" I pleaded, desperate now. "This has gone more than far enough!!"

"You know, I just thought of something." David said to Alex, straightening his tie for him.

"What's that?" Alex asked.

"Seeing as the boss man is all tied up and ripe for some more action, lets tell a few of those faggot bellboys about him before we get to the hotel conference room." David said mockingly. "I'm sure they'd like to get their mouths on those meaty executive tits of his…"

"Sounds like a plan to me!" Alex laughed as they headed for the room door.

"Oh, and don't worry your handsome head over the meeting Boss man." David said mockingly, looking back at me. "We'll take notes for you…"

Laughing, they exited the room, closing and locking the door behind them.

Shit!!" I yelled in total anger and utter frustration.

I looked down at my sore nipples and my semi hard dick.

"Fuck!!" I seethed.

As I sat there thinking about all that the two bellboys went on and on eating my nipples with pure delight and super gusto. At that point I thought about the first two bellboys who had come to the room, not too long after Alex and David had left...

It was about fifteen minutes or so later and I was *still* trying desperately to get myself untied. I was soaked with sweat by then and stinking of it too. If I did manage to get myself untied I would have to shower before heading to the meeting. Then, I heard the sound of a key in the door of the room. I looked over at the door and saw two bellboys enter.

"Oh shit," I whispered and gulped hard in fear.

"Good afternoon Ralph," the first bellboy, a tall young guy with wavy brown hair said to me as he approached me.

He and his friend, another young guy but shorter than he with darker brown hair squatted down at my sides as I sat there, feeling totally helpless.

"Can't fucking believe this shit," the first bellboy said, hooking one hand around my upper leg and his other hand around my socked ankle at the side of me that he was squatting at. "Those two guys' weren't fucking kidding. There really is a handsome executive dude all roped up in here and ready to be eaten like crazy."

"Yeah, he sure as fuck is," the other bellboy said, squatting at my other side.

The second bellboy took my dick in his fist, stroked it, and loudly slurped one of my sore nipples into his mouth.

"Ayyyyrrr shit, perverts, you two also!!" I gasped.

The first bellboy licked my other nipple as he ran his hand up and down over my socked ankle, playing with my tied foot.

"Fucking bastards, better untie me when you're done having your fun." I said threateningly. "I intend to let the hotel management know about this shit!! I am a banking executive after all."

As the second bellboy stroked me and slurped heartily at my nipple I felt myself getting ready to shoot a second hefty load of creamy spunk.

"Ohhhhrr shit, God, *this can't be fucking happening!!"* I ranted breathlessly and squirmed helplessly under the binding ropes. "Alex and David *will* pay for this shit!! Ohhhhrrrr shit!!"

The two bellboys took their mouths off my nipples and I shot a second load of executive jizz all over myself, just as I had earlier. Big thick creamy ropes of it erupted from my dick slit, splattering all over me, again soaking the ropes holding me to the chair and dripping down to my stomach area.

"Fuck, never saw a guy shoot so much sperm," the first bellboy said as his buddy went on stroking me some more. "He must really enjoy being tied up like this."

"Ayyyyrrr shit, enough already!!" I gasped, as my super sensitive dick remained trapped in the bellboy's fist as he stroked every possible drop from me.

"Man, a real sweet treat for us," the first bellboy said enthusiastically, his tongue practically sticking out of his mouth.

"Yeah, but lets really sweeten it up first," the second bellboy said, jumped to his feet, and pulled his hard and pulsing dick from his uniform pants.

His buddy followed suit and then I was sitting there watching the two young bellboys slowly stroke their big, throbbing tube steaks, aimed directly at my cum soaked chest area. The first bellboy's dick was long, fat, and had a thick foreskin on it. For whatever the reason, watching him stroke that big meat with that foreskin sliding back and forth on it was getting my dick hard all over again. I looked at his dick in awe, not realizing that I was doing so...

"Like this dick of mine eh Ralph?" the first bellboy asked me. "Yeah, I know how it is. Even you straight boys are amazed at this meat of mine."

My breath came in short gasps as he stroked that big dick closer to me. His buddy tweaked one of my nipples hard as he went on stroking himself on the other side of me. When the first bellboy was close enough to me I could fuckin' smell the sweat on his foreskin. Now I did stick out my tongue. Teasing me, he placed the tips of two of his fingers to my lips. I sniffed heartily and licked his fingers; the taste from his big dick foreskin was salty and musty all at once.

"Ohhhh you fucking bastards," I whispered as he stroked his dick against my shoulder. "Perverts, making me crazy..."

I leaned my head back and looked up at the two young men as they brought themselves closer and closer to eruption. Leaning my head back stretched my bound chest area out erotically in the chair.

"Ohhhhrr man, I'm getting there now man," the second bellboy panted. "Fuck man, seeing that dick of yours with that funky foreskin always makes me hornier than a bitch in heat, but this roped up executive boy really puts the icing on the fucking cake..."

"I know what you mean buddy, ohhh fuck, ohhhrr yeah," the first bellboy panted as well.

The two young bellboys shot their thick, creamy loads all over my chest and stomach areas, mixing their juices with mine.

"Ohhhhrr shit, ohhh fuckin' A!!!" the first bellboy gasped as he stroked himself like crazy, his dick and foreskin glistening with his cum.

He saw me looking hungrily at that dick of his and again placed two fingers to my lips. I lapped greedily at his cum-soaked fingers, sucking at them like crazy. Then the bastard took his fingers away and the two bellboys again hunkered down at my sides. They licked their cum and mine slowly off me, slurping at my nipples in between licks. I was covered with goose bumps and sweating like crazy as the first bellboy stroked my again hard dick as they went on licking me as if I was an ice cream cone. They stroked another good sized load out of me before finally standing up, packing their dicks back into their uniform pants, and heading for the hotel room door.

"Fuckers, *untie me*!!" I ranted demandingly as they were about to leave.

"Sorry Ralph, we were told we could have our fun with you but we were not to untie you, no matter what," the first bellboy said and then they were gone.

"Damn it!!" I ranted angrily. "Damn it all!!"

I again began trying to get myself untied…

As I thought back on all this the two bellboys that were now in my room were *still* slurping and licking at my nipples like crazy… I chewed helplessly and in frustration on my sock gag as the bellboy with the dark hair stroked my sore dick as he and his buddy went on and on eating my nipples like crazy…

"RRRRmmmmffff!!!!" I sputtered angrily, feeling myself getting close to shooting yet another hefty sized load of executive jizz.

And then, sure enough, I came again like gangbusters, spraying a good hot load of sperm all over myself.

"RRRRmmmmfff…" I gasped breathlessly.

The two bellboys, their mouths now off my nipples watched as I shot rope after rope of cum all over myself.

"Shit, guy cums like a bandit," one of the bellboys said mockingly. "Wonder if his wife gets him off like this."

I looked down at them angrily, grimacing meanly through my sock gag…

A little while later the two bellboys were gone and I was again alone in the room, still tied up and pretty helpless... At least they had taken the sock gag out of my mouth before leaving my room. The socks that had been used to gag me were on the floor, next to one of my bound feet, my saliva glistening on them. I was a stinking mess of sweat, cum, and bellboy saliva. I glanced at the digital clock on one of the bedside tables and saw that I had been tied up for more than an hour at that point. If I got myself untied I would still be able to make the meeting, seeing as the meetings usually went on for a little more than two hours. I took a deep breath and again began struggling like a wild man in the chair.

"Ohhhhrrr shit!!!" I grunted. "Come on Ralph, you fuckin' work out constantly!! You're strong as a bull!! Shouldn't be a fucking problem getting these ropes untied!!"

After a while of really struggling I was still unable to get myself untied. Shit!! My dick was again hard as a rock and sticking out of my boxer shorts, pointing straight up at the ceiling, oozing droplets of pre cum. I looked down at it and it seemed to be mocking me, telling me that it knew me better than I knew myself. As I sat there looking down at my hard dick, still struggling to get untied, I heard a key in the hotel room door.

"Oh shit," I muttered as I saw the knob on the door turning. *"Not again..."*

The door opened and when I saw two of the account representatives from the toy manufacturing company that is based in New York City come in I gulped loud and hard, embarrassment filling me.

"Shit," I whispered, vowing inwardly that I would kill Alex and David for this.

After locking the door to the hotel room John and Abe strode over to me, snide expressions on both their handsome faces.

"Uh, hi guys," I said, embarrassment filling me as my dick stuck straight up, long and hard, seeming to look at the two corporately dressed men.

A glob of pre cum oozed to the tip of my dick slit and slid down the sides of it. The two men were looking hungrily at my manhood.

"Well Ralph, it would certainly appear that you have gotten yourself stuck in what is often referred to as a sticky wicket," John, a very tall man in his early forties with salt and pepper colored hair said to me with a mean looking grin on his face.

Abe, a man slightly shorter than John in his late thirties with dark brown wavy hair and a thick mustache stepped behind me and placed a hand on the back of my neck.

"Yeah, and he sure as shit does look real fucking hot all roped up the way he is," Abe said to John, stroking and squeezing the back of my neck as he spoke. "Not a fucking thing he can do to stop us from having some real sick fun with him huh John?"

"I agree totally, and I truly am so glad that Alex and David clued us in on this."

The two men shucked off their suit jackets, loosened their ties, and rolled up their sleeves.

"Uh guys, look, I don't know what you two have in mind for me *but* I sure as hell would appreciate it if you would untie me," I said as the two men squatted at my sides.

"Tell me Ralph, do you enjoy being the chief executive of our companies account with your bank?" John asked me, reaching forward and giving one of my sore nipples a hard squeeze.

"Y-yeah, sure, you know I do," I said, grimacing miserably as he squeezed my nipple harder, twisting it meanly between his big thick fingers.

"Well then, if you wish to continue managing that account you'll just deal with what's happening here at the moment," John said sternly. "When we speak on the phone again next week none of this will be spoken of or even remembered. Is that clear?"

Looking down, I watched as John fingered the nipple he had between his fingers and I'll be damned I thought as I saw Abe hunkered down and leaning over one of my tied feet. Fucking guy was kissing and licking the tip of my shoe and running his hand up and down my socked calf. My dick was rage hard between my legs, aching and begging to shoot yet another load of my executive jizz.

"Oh fuck, go ahead you guys," I muttered. "Go ahead and fuckin' work on me…"

Abe sat up and the two men smiled at each other. Then, John reached into the fly opening of my boxers and hooked his fingers tightly around the prizes he sought in there. I clenched my teeth in pain as John brought my big hairy, sweaty, and stinking balls out of the fly opening in my boxer shorts. With his fingers he grabbed one of my nuts and squeezed it hard. Abe followed suit by grabbing my other nut and squeezing that one also.

"Ohhhrrr good God, shit you guys, not my balls," I grunted. "Fucking poor things are so sore after being drained like crazier earlier."

They pulled hard on my balls, stretching them, tugging them painfully. My hard dick twitched back and forth as my nuts were out rightly tortured. I grunted miserably and grimaced in a mixture of pain and pleasure as my two business clients tortured the fuck out of my balls. I could not believe this shit was happening and all because I had lost at a fucking card game. Next time we would play for money I thought. Then, to my utter surprise and total shock the two men that I always thought were as straight as I leaned forward and they each slurped one of my pulsing and aching balls into their mouths.

"Ayyyyyyrrr GOD!!!" I gasped and threw my head back as they slurped, sucked, and really put the pressure to my balls with their tongues. "Guys, please, no, not this!! Arrrrrhhh shit, get to admit though it does feel pretty good at that!!"

As John and Abe sucked my balls like crazy I heard the hotel room door open. I looked over and saw Alex and David entering the room.

"Fuckers," I seethed. "Just look at what you two have gotten me into!!"

They quickly shucked off their suit jackets, dashed over to me, squatted at my sides near John and Abe and slurped one of my nipples each into their mouths.

"Ohhhhhhrrr fucks," I panted. "Fuckin' four of you feasting on me now like I was a damned buffet or something!!"

I squirmed and writhed in the chair, sweating and grunting as the four men treated me like a cheap whore. Abe ran his hand up and over my socked calf a few times as he went on and on sucking my nut that was swelling up in his mouth.

"Ohhhhhhrrr you fuckers," I gasped.

I threw my head back again when John's hand closed around my pulsing and super hard dick. All it took was three good pulls and I was spewing a good-sized mess of executive jizz all over my stomach area.

"Ayyyyrrr yeah, yeah you fuckers, got me creaming again like a bitch in heat," I swore.

When I was done spewing my mess John and Abe let my aching balls slip from their mouths and Alex and David stopped working my nipples. The four men stood up and stood around me. I watched as they all unzipped their suit pants and brought out their big hard and pulsing dicks. They aimed their dicks at me and began stroking themselves, the four of them grunting and groaning in pleasure at the sight of the bound and very used up executive.

"Oh man, four of you going to spew your messes all over me huh?" I panted. "Yeah, go for it you fuckers; let me see what you got!!"

It was Abe that spurted first, shooting a good sized load of cream all over my chest and nipples, followed by John who also shot a hefty sized load of executive jizz all over me. David and Alex came together, shooting their loads onto my chest and nipples also. Man, did I need a shower, as I smelled more than ripe at that moment. For a fleeting moment I thought of my wife and thought if she could see me now...

The four men standing around me caught their breath as I sat there with my soft dick and aching balls hanging between my legs and an enormous mess of jizz caking up all over my chest and stomach areas.

"Well gentlemen, I want to thank you both for a very productive meeting and a very interesting encounter," John said to Alex and David. "It's good to know that we'll be here for a few more days."

The four men chortled heartily and a look of utter dismay came over my face. They all packed their dicks back into their suit pants.

"Are you going to untie him now?" Abe asked Alex and David.

"Eventually," Alex replied and all the men laughed again.

They all shook hands and John and Abe left the room, Abe taking my socks that had been used to gag me earlier by two of the bellboys. Fuck, stealing a guy's socks has to be one of the top ten perverted things you can do.

"You bastards," I said to Alex and David through clenched teeth. "I swear I should fire both your asses!!"

"On what charge Boss man?" Alex asked me, stepping behind me and stroking my hair. "You agreed to the rules of the game after all."

"I agreed to the rules of the game," I said angrily. "I did not however agree to be used as a sexual buffet for faggots!!"

"Hey, you can look at that as a bonus," David said merrily, squatted down in front of me and ran the palms of his hands over my socked calves. "I mean, you *did* get your rocks off a few times."

Looking down at David stroking my calves and toying with my black socks I managed a wicked looking grin.

"Fuck man, get me off again then untie me you sleazy fucks!" I said slyly. "Then I want a rematch on that damned card game."

My two work associates eagerly squatted at my sides, slurped my nipples into their mouths, and took turns stroking my again hard dick…

A little while later I was (finally, finally) untied from the chair and the three of us were sitting at the table as I dealt the cards. I was still wearing just my shoes, socks, and boxer shorts.

"Are you sure you want to do this Boss man?" Alex asked me. "I mean, what if you lose again? The rules still apply you know."

"I know," I said, looking across at him intensely. *"The rules still apply and this time I do not intend to lose…"*

Alas, fate was not on my side that day, not at all. It took about ten minutes but even at that point I knew I was losing the game. I cursed and swore under my breath every time I lost another round. My dick twitched in fear in my boxer shorts.

"Good thing you didn't bother to get dressed boss man," Alex said to me, reaching over and giving one of my nipples a hard squeeze.

"Bastards," I seethed as I sat there looking at what was left of my cards.

I stole a glance over at the chair I had been tied to. The mounds of rope were still on the floor around the chair.

"Shit, shit…" I said miserably.

When the game was over Alex and David didn't waste any time. They had me back in that chair and roped up right fast… They hunkered at my sides, feasting like crazy on my sore nipples and taking turns stroking my big hard crank…

Needless to say I spent a good amount of time roped to that chair on that business trip. You see, each time I stupidly challenged Alex and David to another game of cards I lost…

ROOKIE COP ABDUCTION

The alarm clock went off at four AM, or should I say the alarm clock jangled at four AM. I opened my eyes and still more asleep than awake I reached over a muscular arm and slammed my ham-like hand down on the button atop the thing, silencing it. I grunted a few times and then sat up, swinging my muscular tree-trunk like legs off the bed, resting my big feet on the floor. Sitting there with a piss hard on in my briefs I rubbed the sleep from my eyes and ran my hands over the top of my head a few times, scratching it. I groggily walked to the bathroom in just my tented white briefs to shower and shave the start of another long and hot August day in New York City. Little did I know however just what that particular day had in store for me. In the bathroom I turned on the light, allowed my eyes to adjust to it while I stood there squinting and I shucked off my briefs. I turned on the water in the shower and stepped under the luke-warm spray. As I soaped myself all over my cock was more than rigid and hard, jutting out all beefy, long and fat in front of me, all eight and a half inches of the guy. I would have jacked myself off good and fucking proper but for whatever the reason that morning I didn't touch my big beefy hard on. Perhaps I somehow and instinctively knew that I would need my energy for later in the day. I did however piss long, hard and yellow in the shower. I know that most dudes out there wouldn't admit to doing something like that, but hey, what the fuck? Most guys piss in the shower whether they want to admit it or not. A girl I dated a while back thought it was absolutely revolting. Pissing when you have a big raging hard-on feels almost as good as shooting a whopper of a load let me tell you. Well, maybe not *exactly,* but it sure does feel good. When I was done in the bathroom I walked naked back to my bedroom to get dressed. I flicked on the light in the bedroom and there it was. At the sight of my police rookie uniform hanging outside my closet my heart swelled with the utmost pride bud. I was on my way to becoming one of New York's finest. With a smile of total pride I pulled on fresh white briefs and a pair of knee length black nylon wide ribbed dress socks. With a new hard-on beginning in my fresh briefs I took my uniform off its hanger and got dressed, beginning with my shirt, buttoning it up slowly, reverently it seemed over my massively muscled torso. Moments later I looked in awe at my reflection in the full-length mirror. Gray button down shirt pressing tightly against my muscular chest and massive pecs, black tie tied perfectly into a Windsor knot, tight navy blue trousers outlining my long muscular legs and beefy calves and showing off my tight round muscular bubble butt. Black patent leather lace-up shoes adorned my big size eleven feet. God, I looked perfect, almost like a real New York City police officer bud. I put my flap hat in my big book bag along with my gym clothes, (for later in the day, or so I thought at that moment) my baton, my notebook, my police training manual and a host of other supplies that I would need when I arrived at the academy. Sadly for me though on that day I would not make it to the academy…

My name is Giordano, Anthony Giordano to be exact. I'm twenty-three years old; I have dark brown (military cut) hair and dark brown eyes. I'm just about all of six feet tall and my body (as I have proudly described to you) is very muscular and well toned since I started training at the academy three months ago. Amazing how fucking fast they get you in shape. I always worked out regularly at the gym, even before signing up at the police academy so I was in reasonably good shape already. But within three months of hardcore workouts at the academy I would say it's suffice to admit that they turned me into a real muscle animal. I had decided to become a New York City police officer because I wanted to be a part of something good. I'm not one of those guys who come from a family where his father was a cop and his grandfather was a cop and his great grandfather was a cop and so on and so on. What I want (and need) to tell you about happened in the hot month of August, when I was put to the hardest test of my life, even harder than my training at the police academy. It was a test of my strength (literally) and my nerves and my stamina and a test to win back the greatest gift of all, my freedom. With my "Police Academy of New York City" monogrammed bag packed I was ready to go. It was Friday, four forty five AM and as I locked up my apartment I was thinking about the weekend and my beautiful girlfriend Cindy. Fucking more than beautiful Cindy who can't get enough of my big Italian sausage I thought with pride. The last time her and I had gotten together my cock was so sore that it was unbelievable. I had fucked her that many times bud. Outside it was still dark, but very hot and humid so I walked slowly toward the subway station. My cock was now semi hard and pulsing in my rookie uniform pants. I couldn't resist smiling at how good that felt let me tell you. Maybe that was why I had decided not to jack off back in the shower that morning. Maybe I wanted that feeling of sleaziness and desire all day. The neighborhood is pretty much deserted at the early hour that I leave the house. (Police academy training starts promptly at six forty five AM.) Being that it's a decent enough neighborhood, low crime rate and all that I never once worried about walking the streets that early to the train station. Actually, I rather enjoyed the walk in the quiet streets, until that particular Friday morning bud. As I was about to cross the second street a big van (it was the size of a medium sized U-haul or a moving truck) suddenly pulled up in front of me, blocking my path. Jeez, I hadn't even heard the roar of the van's engine as it had pulled up near me. I must have still been more asleep than awake at that moment. The guy sitting in the passenger seat rolled down his window and leaned out, looking at me intently.

"Excuse me Officer-er-Rookie Giordano," he said, noticing my rookie uniform and nametag pinned to my shirt. "My friend and I here seem to be lost and we were wondering if you could perhaps help us out with some directions."

He appeared to be pretty big, muscular. He had dark hair and dark sinister looking eyes, yet sort of dopey looking. He was dressed in a tee shirt with denim overalls over it. I guessed him to be a construction worker of some kind. I glanced over at the guy in the driver's seat. He was a lot bigger than his friend in the passenger seat, also with dark hair and dark sinister looking eyes, although he didn't look the least bit dopey. He was also dressed like some kind of a construction worker.

"Where do you need to go?" I asked the guy in the passenger seat, trying to sound as if I was in a hurry, which I was actually.

He smiled, reached into his pocket and brought out a sheet of paper. He showed it to me. On it was written eighty Fifth Street and twenty Third Avenue.

"Eight Fifth Street and twenty Third Avenue," he said as we looked at the paper.

"That's not too far from here at all," I said and raised my arm, pointing my finger in the direction that they should go. "Go straight down Bay Parkway for another ten blocks or so and then turn left and…"

Suddenly, the guy in the passenger seat reached forward and grabbed my outstretched arm with a strong beefy like hand and a tighter than tight grip. He quickly pulled me hard against the van.

"UHHHHHNNNFFFFFF!!!!!" I sputtered as my body slammed into the door of the big van, feeling stunned. "*Wh-wha…*"

"I got him Cleeve!!" the guy cried out triumphantly. "*Shit, I fuckin' got him!!*"

I tried desperately to pull away from his strong vise-like grasp, wondering what the fuck was going on, wondering if this was some kind of sick joke, but he reached his other arm out the window and grabbed me with his other hand as well.

"Let go of me you bastard!!" I roared as I again tried to pull out of his grasp.

"Ready to go for a ride Rookie boy?" he asked me with a mean looking grin.

Suddenly, the guy in the driver's seat pressed his foot against the pedal and the van started moving slowly.

"*H-holy fucking shit!!*" I screeched in a high-pitched tone of voice.

I instantly dropped my book bag on the ground, grabbed the handle on the door of the van and hopped up onto the small ledge on the side of the van.

"Hold on tight Rookie boy," the guy in the passenger seat teased me, holding tight to my arm as the van moved faster. "You did just what I predicted you would do, hopping up there like that. They must train you rookies real well."

As the van picked up speed the guy in the passenger seat held tighter still to my arm as I held onto the door handle for dear life. I glanced back for a moment and watched as my book bag slowly disappeared from my sight as the van moved faster and faster.

"Ohhhhhhhrrr shit man, st-stop, stop the goddamned van!!" I yelled in at the driver.

He had a sadistic looking grin etched across his pursed lips as he drove.

My big feet barely fit on the small ledge and I was sure that I was going to fall off and wind up breaking every bone in my body.

"Hang on Rookie boy!" the guy in the passenger seat said mockingly. "So glad that you decided to join us for the ride."

"What-what the fuck is this all about???" I screamed at them as the van went even faster. "Good God almighty, *please stop!!*"

The driver kept that wicked smile on his face as he expertly drove the van further and further up the long block we were on. The humid air rushed past me and I was a sweaty and grubby mess as I held on and held on. Finally, the van stopped twelve avenues from where they had snagged me. I slowly let go of the door handle and pressed my palm against the side of the van.

"*Fuckers,*" I whispered as I tried to catch my breath. "Wh-what is this, some kind of sick fucking joke?"

"Keep talking like that and we'll take a nice long ride on the highway for a few miles Rookie boy," the driver barked at me. "And at this time of morning the parkway is just about as deserted as these streets. Hold onto him tight Otis."

The driver pressed his foot down on the pedal again and the van started moving.

"Oh jeez, no man, come on give a rookie guy a break here!" I ranted and quickly grabbed the door handle again. "Ohhhhhrrr fucccckkk!!!"

The guy drove faster and faster through the deserted streets as I again held on for dear life, my tie flapping in front of me in the warm morning wind. Fuck, where was a cop when a guy needed one??? What a sick joke that was, seeing as I was on my way to becoming a cop. When the van stopped a second time I again let go of the door handle, but the guy in the passenger seat (whose name was Otis, as I had found out earlier) still held tightly to my arm. The guy in the driver's seat stepped out of the van and as he did I hopped down off the ledge, ready to hop back up there just in case he decided to take me for another spin.

"Fuck, let go of me man!!" I seethed, trying to pull away from Otis.

Just then, the driver came around the side of the van. He was fucking huge, built like a brick shit house to put it plainly. I was ready for him though, at least I thought I was. I was ready to try out the training I had gotten at the academy.

"Good choice as usual Otis," the driver said as he slowly approached me, grinning maniacally from ear to ear, leering at me, practically drooling. "He is more than *fucking hot*. And a rookie cop to bat as well, ha!!"

"H-hey, you two are faggots!!" I roared like a trapped animal. "So that's what this is all about huh? Think you're goin' to live out some sick cop fantasies with me or something?"

As the driver came closer I clenched my free hand into a tight fist.

"Real hot rookie boy you are at that," the driver said and reached for my askew necktie.

"Faggot!!!" I seethed through clenched teeth and quickly raised my fisted hand.

But, as I was about to swing good and fucking hard at him Otis yanked my arm that he was holding and slammed me bodily (and painfully I might add) against the van, stunning the fuck out of me.

He yanked on my arm again and slammed me against the side of the van, *again...*

"Unnnnghhhhhh!!!" I moaned and my head spun.

"Easy Otis, we don't want to ruin him," the driver said, still leering at me and closed his big fingers around the knot in my tie. "He is too perfect to ruin, *just yet.*"

"Whatever you say Cleeve," Otis responded respectfully.

"Wh-what do you guys want?" I asked sheepishly, knowing that my chances against them now were more likely naught.

"We already got it Rookie boy," the man named Cleeve said to me, grinning and tugging on my tie. *"We got you."*

My eyes opened wide in sheer terror...

He let go of my tie and took a pair of handcuffs out of his pocket.

"Wonder how you're going to feel being locked in a pair of handcuffs Rookie boy," Cleeve said devilishly. "You're probably thinking that this should be going the other way around huh?"

"Goddamn you man!!" I seethed, having gotten my bearings at that point.

I again made a meaty fist, prepared to pummel the driver, and at the same time ready to pull out of Otis' goddamned grasp. But that guy Otis, oh man, he was faster than fast bud. It was as if he could read my mind. As I brought my fist up a second time Otis again yanked on my arm that he was holding. He slammed me again, harder this time against the side of the van.

"Hooofffffff!!!" I sputtered, the wind being knocked out of me again.

"We'll hook him up in the back of the van for the ride home Otis," Cleeve said as he calmly locked one of the steel cuffs around my wrist that was outside the van. "We can work him on the way, use him for break stops and all that crap."

Otis slowly and cautiously pushed my other arm toward Cleeve and in seconds my other wrist was cuffed as well, my hands locked in front of me. Shaking in fear in my shoes and socks I looked around desperately for help, but fuck it all (and me) there was no one in sight. I didn't dare yell for help for fear of what these two psychos would do to me if I did.

"Come on Rookie boy, let's get you ready for your ride," Cleeve said and yanked me toward the back of the van by my tie.

"W-wait, what do you guys think you're doing?" I garbled miserably as I stumbled along.

"Otis, get out of the fucking van and help me here," Cleeve said commandingly.

"Fuckers, *kidnapping me,*" I whispered in total and outright fear. "God damn it all you guys, kidnapping a police officer is a federal offense, and the same goes for rookies."

A few minutes later I was standing trapped in the back of the van. My muscular arms were stretched above me and my cuffed hands were hooked to a chain that was welded securely into the ceiling of the vehicle and fuck of all fucks, *I was blindfolded.*

"L-look, I really think that you guys grabbed the wrong man here," I said pleadingly as I felt their big mangy hands moving over me at my sides, my stomach area and under my arms. "I mean I'm not even gay."

"Who the fuck said anything about being gay?" I heard Cleeve ask me tauntingly and the two men laughed sadistically. "We just want to have some nasty fun with you Rookie boy."

I then heard them step out of the back of the van. They rolled the metal door down and it slammed shut. The sound of the door clicking locked filled me with utter dread. I was feeling terrified as the van began moving. Fuck, *this was no joke...*

As the van started moving faster I figured that we were on a parkway. The way we were moving along so fast I had to really rivet myself to stay balanced in the back of that van. I was swerved from side to side a few times and I was sort of thankful that they hadn't tied my feet together. I tried to pull the small chain of the handcuffs off the chain they were attached to, but being blindfolded made that task impossible. Besides, even if I weren't blindfolded the back interior of the van was very dark. After a long while I was sweating profusely, from both the fact that it was miserably hot in the back of the van (no air conditioning for the kidnapped rookie boy bud) and from outright fear. I wondered why these two lunatics had kidnapped me. I wondered what they were planning on doing to me. And I wondered despondently if I would ever see freedom again. Shivering in fear in my sweat sopped uniform shirt I wondered if they were going to kill me. When the van stopped the first time I estimated that we had been rolling along for close to a good hour or so. My arms were horribly numb from being stretched above me for so long. I heard the back door of the van roll open and Cleeve and Otis stepped inside with me.

"Enjoying the ride so far Rookie boy?" Cleeve asked me and tugged playfully on my tie.

"Where the hell are you guys taking me???" I asked, trying to sound as authoritative as possible and not as fear filled as I was really feeling. "I am a rookie police officer and kidnapping a rookie cop is a federal offense, just as if you'd kidnapped a full-fledged cop! This is a total offense!!"

"Only if we get caught Rookie boy," Otis said mockingly and ran his hand over my crotch, sending waves of chills through me.

He then grasped my crotch real tight and I involuntarily hoisted myself to my toes...

"F-fucking perverts," I seethed angrily.

A feeling of total helplessness enveloped me as I felt my pants being undone. They fell down around my ankles and I felt Cleeve and Otis' hands roaming over my white briefs. My cock was hard from fear; at least that's what I thought I was hard from.

"Fucking rookie boy has a hard on the size of a python," Otis said in disbelief.

"Yeah, once we get 'em all trapped and scared they all get that fear hard on," Cleeve said.

Based on what Cleeve had just said I guessed that they had kidnapped other men before me. But why hadn't those men reported it? Did they report it? Somehow I would have to find out, if I got out of this alive that is. Shit, I decided then and there that if I did get out of this alive I would see these two put away for the rest of their lives. It would be my first act as an officer of the law! Suddenly, my thoughts were cut short as I felt my cock and balls being pulled meanly out of the fly opening in my briefs.

"Ohhhhrrrr no, no, not this you guys!!" I blubbered miserably as I wasn't being handled all that gently.

"Yeah, that's right Otis my man, suck that rookie's cock," Cleeve said and then Otis greedily slurped my big hardness into his mouth.

"Ohhhhhhhhhh no, no, *no,*" I whimpered. *"Please not this…"*

I felt Otis' hands roaming over and over my muscular thighs, down my legs and over my knee length black socks. He playfully snapped the elastic in my socks as he sucked my big cock harder and harder, poking his tongue into my piss hole.

"Arrrrrrhhhhhh, y-you bloody perverts," I gasped; trying not to sound like I was enjoying what was being done to me.

Then, Cleeve pulled my briefs down in the back and spread my ass globes apart, exposing my pink stink hole.

"Arrrrrrrrhhhh wh-*what now???*" I seethed, feeling totally mortified.

In response Cleeve plunged his tongue deep into my exposed bunghole. My muscular body bucked forward, involuntarily pushing my cock deeper into Otis' mouth.

"Ohhhhhh fuck, fuck," I moaned as the two men tongued me savagely back and front. The feeling of my ass being eaten was sending shockwaves of thrills and chills through me. As the two men sucked and feasted on me, goose bumps broke out all over my muscular body.

When I was about to cum Otis stopped sucking my cock and ran that big mangy tongue of his over my low hanging nuts, applying pressure to them, and torturing me erotically.

"ARRRRRHHHHHHH!!! Fuck, easy with my family jewels you fucker!!" I ranted.

Otis tongued my balls like crazy, slathering his big tongue all over them like crazy, sucked them alternately and tongued and tongued them hard some more as Cleeve went on and on wildly licking and sucking at my stink hole. I felt his lips pucker against it and he sucked the fuck out of it back there. My head was spinning out of orbit and my muscular hard body was writhing in forced ecstasy. I was more sweating like crazy now as the two men literally feasted on me.

"Damned faggots," I whimpered angrily. "Fuckin' raping me."

Then, Otis gobbled my cock back into his mouth, the feeling as he did so, so abrupt that I nearly jumped out of my shoes, swirled his tongue over and over it a few times and then I felt it bud. *I was going to cum and cum like crazy.*

"Ohhhhhhhhhrrrr God, oh shit, I'm going to fucking shoot my load you bastards!!" I roared and came like a bandit in Otis' mouth. "Arrrrrrhhhh yeahhhhhh!!!!"

I arched my back and leaned my head back between my arms as Otis continued sucking me, milking every possible drop of cum out of my cock, siphoning me almost it felt like. Cleeve continued eating my hole as I seemed to cum and cum and cum…

"Ohhhhhrrrrr shit!!!" I ranted as Otis gulped down my juices. "Fucking milking me like a damned cow!!"

I nearly went crazy though when I realized that Otis *wasn't* going to stop sucking me. He swirled his tongue over my slimy semi hard cock.

"Ohhhhhhhhhh no, no," I pleaded breathlessly and hoisted myself to my toes. Shit man, *pl-please stop,* I'm all sensitive and sexy feeling after I've just popped a big ol' nut."

I hung there feeling totally helpless yet super charged up all at the same fucking time as the two men forced me to then piss, my cock all sensitive feeling as Otis scoffed down my thick yellow mess. My God, even my stink hole was feeling pretty sensitive as Cleeve tongued and tongued the bejesus out of it.

"Ohhhhhhhhrrrrr shhhiiiiiittttt, g-got me pissing down your throat again you perverted bastard!" I panted as I felt as if Otis was using a vacuum pump to siphon my piss from me, his mouth felt that alive around my big throbbing cock.

When I was done pissing Otis let my cock slip out of his mouth and Cleeve stopped lapping at my now saliva soaked stink hole. I felt his saliva dripping liberally out of my hole and down my legs as my cock hung semi hard and all messy and slimy between my tree-trunk like legs.

"He tastes fucking great," Otis said to Cleeve.

"Yeah, and his shit chute is nice and funky," Cleeve said, smacking his lips together. "Let's get moving and when we stop again we'll trade places.

"Sounds good to me," Otis said happily.

"Fuckers, what's the point of all this???" I ranted angrily as I slowly lowered myself flat on my feet again, pulling madly at the handcuffs. Fuckers kidnapped me and now you're fucking raping me!!"

"Rookie boy, we're just getting started on you," Cleeve said as he undid my necktie and pulled it off me. "By the time we're done with you you'll never be the same."

He meanly crammed my tie into my mouth as Otis yanked my fallen pants off me over my shoes and socks.

"RRRRRmmmmmmffff!!!" I sputtered miserably as I was gagged and unceremoniously de-panted.

Then, a few moments later I was again alone in the back of the van as we moved on. My shirt was wide open in the front, unbuttoned and exposing my muscular chest, my cock and balls were sticking out of my briefs, which were also pulled down in the back, just the way Cleeve and Otis had left them. And I was still wearing my shoes and socks. What a fucked up sight I was for a New York City police rookie. I felt a mixture of fear, humiliation and anguish wash over me. As the van plowed on my cock (for whatever the reason) grew rigid and hard again.

A while later (a half hour perhaps by my best estimates) the van stopped again. I heard the metal door rolling up and open, *again*. Then, I felt their big mangy hands all over me, *again,* as Cleeve and Otis pawed me. They squeezed my nipples real hard, twisting and yanking the tender flesh of my poor nubs, pinched the bejeus out of them and twisted and yanked them some more.

"MMMMMFFFF!!!!" I wailed as they tortured the fuck out of my poor nipples.

"Nice tits on him eh Otis?" Cleeve asked.

"Yeah, nice and ripe for torturing," Otis said and then the two men each slurped one of my nipples into their mouths.

"Mmmmmmmmm…"I suddenly crooned as they sucked, bit, chewed, and kissed, fuck, *they kissed my nipples.* "Mmmmmffffff!!!"

Now to tell it plainly my girlfriend had never gone near my nipples and I had never known just how fucking great it could feel to have them worked on, under better circumstances of course. As Cleeve and Otis worked on my tortured nipples my cock grew harder and harder. I fleetingly thought how I would have to get my girlfriend to work some magic on my nipples…when I was out of this mess that is. The two men ran their big hands over and over my chest, my pecs and sides as they continued slurping feverishly, almost as if they were in a trance on my nipples. My God, never before had I been so much aware of my nipples bud. When my poor nipples were more than red, sore and *very erect* and pointy they stopped working them.

"Okay Otis, this time you take his asshole and I'll milk that cock of his," Cleeve said.

"RRRRMMMFFFF!!!!" I sputtered angrily as I felt my ass cheeks being spread apart by Otis this time.

Fuckers, they were using me like I was an object or something…

Then, all at once Otis plunged his tongue into my hole as Cleeve gulped and gobbled my hard cock into his eager mouth. He slathered his tongue over it a few times and then jammed his lips tightly around my shaft. As he got my meat stick situated in his mouth I nearly jumped out of my shoes and socks, the sensations were like lightning coursing through me. The two men started working me together in a rhythmic way, driving me into a further frenzy. Cleeve sucked me like a man possessed as Otis' tongue flicked around in my hole like crazy. Sweat rolled off me everywhere as the two men again feasted on me like I was a damned buffet. I felt Cleeve's hands roaming over my legs, over my socks and over my shoes. He stopped sucking my cock a few times to run his tongue over my sweaty and mangy balls, applying pressure to them like Otis had done earlier. When he meanly gobbled my hardness back into his mouth for the last time I felt it again bud. I was about to shoot yet another man sized load of hot rookie cop jizz. But there was no warning the bastard as I was gagged this time.

"RRRmmmmmmffff!!!" I bantered wildly, arching my back as I shot my big creamy load down Cleeve's throat. "MMMFFFFF!!!!"

As I came and came again Otis went on licking my hole like crazy, sucking on the walls of it and kissing it hard. *Fuck, the guy was kissing my goddamned asshole!* He slapped my muscular butt cheeks hard as Cleeve swallowed every damned drop of my jizz. He squeezed my sore balls, trying to force more and more of my creamy mess out of me. I sputtered in anguish when my cock became more than super sensitive, but he still went on sucking it. I thought I would go totally crazy at that point but finally, Cleeve let my semi hard and now very slimy cock slip slowly out of his mouth as Otis stopped eating my damned hole.

"You're right Otis, he tastes fucking great," Cleeve said.

"Yeah and his shit chute is as funky as you said," Otis agreed. "Man, we are going to have more than a lot of fun with this rookie boy."

They squeezed my nipples hard and laughed meanly s I grimaced miserably and in pain behind the blindfold. I had just found out how very sensitive a guy's nipples can become after he's shot a load or two.

"Come on, let's get home," Cleeve said. "Rookie boy has a lot to look forward to."

They left me alone again and at that point I thought for sure that I would freak out. As the van began moving I was sweating profusely in fear and droplets of cum were dripping from my piss slit. I felt saliva dripping freely out of my hole and my cock grew hard, *again.* My nipples were stinging and felt so sore; actually they felt like they needed more attention, like they needed to be worked on some more. My hard cock felt frustrated at not being made to shoot another load. I had somehow been driven into what I'll call over sensitization.

"Mmmmmmmffff..." I sputtered softly as I wondered what the fuck was happening to me.

Finally, the van came to a stop after pulling up and parking. I was jostled around a bit as the van was slid into what I guessed was a parking space of some kind. Cleeve and Otis stepped up into the back, undid the chain holding the handcuffs above me and lowered my still cuffed hands in front of me. My legs were aching from standing for so long in one spot and my arms felt numb as the two men guided me out of the van. I felt a warm breeze caress me as we exited the back of the van. Where the fuck were we that these two guys could take me out of the van so scantily dressed and with my cock and balls and rear end on total display? When we were all out of the van and standing on the ground Cleeve pulled my tie out of my mouth and took the blindfold off me.

"Take a look Rookie boy," Cleeve said to me with total authority in his voice as my eyes adjusted back to the light. "Take a good fucking look."

I squinted a few times and stared straight ahead at one of the biggest, grandest looking houses I had ever seen. The two men squeezed my exposed butt cheeks and toyed with my hard cock, twisting and spinning it as I took in my surroundings. I grunted and gasped as they played me like a musical instrument. Talk about feeling over sensitized huh bud? God almighty, there wasn't another house around for what seemed like miles and miles. No wonder they could have me out here in broad daylight the way I was practically totally stripped. The house was mansion-like and utterly surrounded by nothing but woods, miles upon miles of woods.

"Y-you guys own this?" I asked them nervously.

"I do," Cleeve replied. "And for a while I want to share it with you Rookie boy."

I gulped hard.

"This will be the hardest test of your life Rookie," Cleeve went on, his strong palm holding a handful of one of my sexy butt cheeks. "Harder than what the hell they put you guys through at the academy. If you survive all that we're going to put you through you'll have earned back your freedom, not to mention the freedom to be a New York City police officer."

Standing there in my shoes and socks, my pulled down briefs and unbuttoned shirt and as Cleeve spoke I looked in awe at the giant house and wondered just what it contained within its immense walls. How in the world did a construction worker own all this? I mean, I knew that these construction type guys made good money and all that, but to be able to afford a mansion-like house all by itself in a remote wooded area? Who was Cleeve???

"And I can tell from the look in your eyes when we captured you that being a New York City police officer more than likely means the world to you Rookie boy," Cleeve went on, telling me about the challenge that I would have to endure to win back my freedom, not giving me any choice *whatsoever* in the matter.

Who was Cleeve???

Moments later I was strewn across Cleeve and Otis' shoulders, being carried into the house…

"God damn it, shit!!! Put me down you fuckers!!" I roared angrily, feeling totally helpless and like a sack of dirty laundry as I was carried into the house.

They lugged me down to a basement, over to a wooden post set right in the center of the room and quickly and expertly roped me tightly to it. As they tied me I looked around the basement and saw that it was actually made up more like a dungeon of sorts, a torture dungeon. To put it another way, it looked like something out of a movie about medieval days. I gulped hard, twice…

"Oh shit man, oh more than fucking shit, you guys really did kidnap the wrong guy," I said desperately as I looked wild-eyed around the basement. "I am not into *any* of this shit."

"Don't worry Rookie boy, you'll learn," Cleeve said and ran the tip of a finger over my quivering lips, squeezing one of my nipples at the same time. "You will learn a lot Rookie boy."

"Otis, squatting down quickly got my big feet tied up to the post, gave my fear hard cock a few quick teasing sucks and stood up next to Cleeve. The two men looked me over appraisingly and hungrily.

"Perfect, absolutely fucking perfect," Cleeve said with an evil grin spread across his face. "So fucking perfect. Come on Otis, let's go upstairs and give Rookie boy here a while to get used to his surroundings."

"No, *no, Oh God no!!!*" I roared and struggled against the tight and binding ropes. "Don't leave me alone down here!!"

But Cleeve and Otis simply ignored me and disappeared up the stairs, closing the basement door behind them.

"Shit, shit, shit!!!" I seethed in a mixture of anger and outright fear. *"Fuck, fuck, I'm goin' to freak out here. Fuck, I've been kidnapped, a cop's worst nightmare, and God, I'm not even a cop yet, just a goddamned rookie boy..."*

Standing there helplessly roped up to the post I looked around the room. I realized with a sick certainty that they had tied me at the most focal point of the entire room. On a wall were hung various types of whips and leather paddles. On shelves I saw transparent storage boxes filled with devices such as dildos, ball separators, and metal ball bearings on strings, butt plugs and a host of other torturous looking devices. Now, I realize that for some people these devices that I'm describing here are erotic and can be used for hours of kinky fun. But I'm not one of those people, when it comes to my sex life I'm a traditional and very vanilla sort of guy. GOD! Against a wall on the other side of the basement I saw what looked like a real but old-fashioned rack. My breath came in short gasps and my stomach lurched and I looked up to keep from vomiting. I then wished I hadn't looked up for hung from the ceiling I saw that there were various hooks attached to pulleys and heavy-duty rope. What the fuck had I fallen into???

A while later Cleeve and Otis came back down the stairs. They were both dressed in black leather shorts, black leather construction boots with white sweat socks tucked down into them and black leather harnesses across their massive chests.

"Oh shit," I whispered as they descended the stairs and made their way over to me.

"Well Rookie boy, what do you think of the play room?" Cleeve asked me and squeezed one of my nipples hard and twisted it, all the while I seemed to be drinking in the sight of his overly erect sexy man nipples.

"YOWWWWWW!!!" I howled in pain. "Pl-play room??? Play room??? This is a fucking torture chamber; it's a room of horrors!"

"You are sooooo fucking right Rookie boy," Cleeve whispered, his fingers still holding tight to my nipple as he leaned in so close to me that our lips were less than an inch apart.

Holding my nipple he again squeezed it hard and before I could yell out a second time in pain I felt it. Glancing down I saw that Otis was on his knees and sucking my hard cock. The greedy mangy bastard had slurped my sausage-sized guy into his mouth so fast that it actually seemed to disappear down in his craw.

"Uhhhhhhhhh…" I breathed deeply and leaned my head back. "Fuckin' sucking my damned sausage again."

"That's it Otis, suck that rookie boy's cock," Cleeve said and squeezed and teased my poor nipple again. "Milk him like a goddamned cow, milk him good."

As Otis feverishly sucked my cock, running his mangy hands up and down my legs Cleeve walked over to the wall where the whips and paddles were hung. He chose a thin riding crop and slowly came back over to me.

"You fucking bastard!" I heaved miserably in the forced ecstasy as my cock was sucked and Cleeve ran the tip of the riding crop over my sore and pointy nipples.

"Those tits of yours look pretty sore Rookie boy," Cleeve said, voicing how I felt as he teased the tips of my nipples with the tip of the riding crop.

The thing felt stinging and sharp against the very tips of my poor sore nipples.

"Please don't," I pleaded as Otis went on and on sucking me.

"After this they'll be more than sore," Cleeve said and raised the riding crop.

He brought it down hard on one of my nipples.

"YOWWWWRRRR!!!" I screamed as searing pain shot through me at what felt to be one hundred miles an hour.

Cleeve wasted no time though. He raised the riding crop again and brought it down again on the same nipple.

"AYYYYYRRRRR!!!!" I screamed, louder this time.

Again he whacked my nipple with the riding crop, again I screamed in a man's agonizing pain and again and again he whacked the same nipple. Each time he whacked my poor nipple I screamed in bloody and tortured agony, but not once did Otis stop sucking my big man meat *and* not once did it go soft in his mouth. Cleeve gave my sore, aching and stinging nipple a final super hard whack with the riding crop and then stepped over to the other one.

"Uhhhhhhhhhh no, no, *please man,*" I begged, tears welling up in my eyes. "Fuck it all man, this is a lousy thing to be doing to a rookie police officer."

But Cleeve simply ignored me and rapped my other nipple hard with the tip of the riding crop.

"AYYYYhhhhh!!!" I screeched in pain and felt it.

I was about to shoot my load again. As Cleeve whacked my other nipple over and over till the pain was blinding and maddening I shot another load into the mindless Otis' mouth. The greedy fuck swallowed every damned drop of my rookie cop juices again as Cleeve went on whacking my nipple harder and harder with each blow. Fuck, the mixture of the pleasure and intense pain was indescribable let me tell you. I felt like I was floating on a cloud between reality and a dream state.

"Ohhhhhhhrrr fuckers!!! Miserable perverts!!" I roared as pain and ecstasy shot through me at the same time. *"Fucking sadists!!!"*

My upper body bucked and squirmed under the tight binding ropes, my muscles straining, dripping in sweat, my head arched halfway back, my lips quivering, my mouth drooling as my cock deposited its load in Otis' gullet....

"OHHHHHHHHHHHHH!!!!!!" I groaned.

When I was done shooting my load Otis let my cock slip out of his mouth and Cleeve stopped whacking my nipple with the riding crop. I stood there roped to the post, more than sweating like crazy at that point, sweating profusely actually, my head hung down, trying to catch my breath. Tears flowed freely from my eyes and landed on the floor at my tied feet. Beat a guy's nipples with a riding crop, how fucked up and sick is that?

"B-bastards," I said breathlessly. "Wh-why are you doin' this to me???"

As I somehow caught my breath the two men tweaked my now very wounded nipples. I yelped and screeched in pain and my head snapped up straight. I couldn't even bear to look at the shape my poor nipples were in.

"Otis, go and get a riding crop," Cleeve said. "Let's really lay into our rookie boy here."

With my tears flowing I looked at Cleeve in utter and total disbelief, and then watched as Otis helped himself to a riding crop like the one Cleeve was holding. The two men then took position at my sides, swinging the riding crops, beating my stomach area over and over, my chest, and my muscular arms and wide shoulders, making sure to connect with my poor nipples from time to time.

"ARRRRRRRHHHHHHH!!!! You fucking bastards!!" I cried loudly and agonizingly.

With looks of glee and determination on their faces they beat my upper body horribly with the riding crops, sending stinging pain soaring through my very being.

"AYYYYYYYRRRR!!!!" I screamed when Cleeve's riding crop connected twice in succession with one of my poor raw nipples. *"Shit, shit, shit!!!!"*

When they stopped a good while later my stomach area, chest and arms were all striped red from the whipping I had just endured. I stood there crying profusely, sweating and stinking with it and my teeth clenched at the injustice of what I was being forced to endure. I strained mightily and in vain against the binding ropes. Cleeve stepped up close to me and grabbed one of my aching nipples.

"This is all just a warm-up Rookie boy," he spat at me, his breath hot on my face. "Wait until we get to the real fun."

Before he could step away from me I spit hard in his face. He smiled insanely, ran a fingertip through my thick saliva as it dripped down his cheek and sucked it into his mouth.

"As I said Rookie boy, you taste good," Cleeve said and suddenly grabbed my chin in his bear like hand.

"OWWWWW!!!!" I yelped.

He squeezed my chin hard, forcing my mouth wide open.

"AHHHHHHHHH!!!!" I cried and Cleeve spit a large wad of phlegm into my open mouth.

He then squeezed my mouth shut, gut punched me and that forced me to swallow the rancid phlegm.

"HUUUFFFFF!!!!" I grunted miserably.

"You'll learn Rookie boy," Cleeve said menacingly. "Even if you have to learn the hard fucking way, *you will fucking learn.*"

Then, Cleeve turned his face to Otis and I saw that he smiling more than manically.

"Otis, I think a good hard lesson is needed for our rookie boy here," Cleeve said, gesturing with his eyes at a cabinet a few feet from where we were all standing. "Would you agree?"

"As you would say Cleeve, sure as shit," Otis responded.

I watched as Cleeve not so gently packed my cock and balls back into my underpants and patted the bulge they made. Then, shaking with glee Cleeve gave one of my nipples a fast tweak and the two men stepped away from me and over to the cabinet that Cleeve had just indicated. My breath came again in short gasps. My soft cock felt all slimy in my briefs. From the cabinet they took a small metal box with holes in it and as far as I could see a container of some kind of white powder. With the back of my head pressed against the post and a look of total and sheer terror in my eyes I watched as the two men stepped back over to me.

"Wh-what now?" I asked through my trembling lips as they took position again at my sides.

Cleeve nodded, smiling at Otis…

Otis took the lid off the container and I curiously saw that it had three small holes in the top of it. He held the container under my nose for a few seconds and I realized that what I was sniffing was grated Parmesan cheese.

"Wh-what the fuck is that for?" I asked.

Without a word Otis yanked the front section of my briefs forward and started sprinkling the grated cheese into them, coating my cock, my balls and my thick pubic bush with the stuff.

"Hey, wh-what's the point of this???" I barked in a squeaky tone of voice, my mind already reeling.

Then, Otis let my waistband on my briefs snap back against my skin in front, stepped to my side and did the same thing with the back section of my briefs, sprinkling grated cheese into them over my ass cheeks. Being that I was all sweaty the grated cheese really stuck to my private areas bud. I started stinking real badly, like some sort of cheap ass Italian restaurant that had failed inspection…

When my underpants were thickly filled with grated cheese I was itchy as hell, but that wasn't to be the worst part of it. Looking at Cleeve Otis said,

"He's ready." Cleeve opened the metal box with the holes in it that he was holding, reached in and brought out a baby white mouse, holding it by the tail...

My heart pounded in mortal fear and my eyes opened wide in sheer and total terror.

"So is this little guy," Cleeve said. "Ready, that is. Poor thing hasn't eaten for two days."

"OH FUCK!!!!!" I screamed insanely as the mouse dangled in Cleeve's fingers, sniffing it seemed down at the cheesy scent emanating from my underpants. "No, oh Good God almighty, *no!!!!!!*"

Otis again pulled my briefs forward in the front and this time Cleeve dropped the baby mouse in them. The little critter landed atop my soft cock and Otis let my briefs snap forward, encasing the hungry rodent in them...

"Hyyyyyyyyyyyyy!!!!" was the sound I made as the thing started scurrying around in my briefs, its tiny claws scratching my cock head as it ate the grated cheese in there. "OHHHHHHHHHRRRR you sick fucks, you bastards from *Hell!!!!!*"

Looking down with my chest jutted out under the tight ropes I watched the sick movement occurring in my briefs as the baby mouse made its way around in there. I felt it struggling through my nest of pubic hair, gulping down cheese as it went.

"G-get it out of there, *Oh god, its goin' to bight my cock you guys!!*" I cried shrilly.

Tears streamed down my face at the inhumanity of this. The mouse found its way then down to my balls, nipping and bighting at my underpants as it went. It seemed frustrated being encased in there yet happy that it was eating the grated cheese. My cock started growing fear hard. The rodent seemed to settle against my slimy and slicked balls and I could feel its mouth eating the cheese off them. Cleeve and Otis watched in total merriment as I suffered, mostly mentally... Cleeve lovingly squeezed my chin a few times as he spoke next.

"Come on Otis, lets go have something to eat as well while Rookie boy here thinks about what's going to happen to him during the next round," Cleeve said, stroking my tear soaked chin and looking down, watching as the mouse started moving again in the confines of my briefs.

I watched in trepidation as the mouse was finding its way up my hard throbbing cock...

Cleeve let go of my chin and he and Otis put the container and the metal box away and hung the riding crops back up on the wall. I could no longer speak, watching in outright horror as the mouse seemed to settle atop my cock head...My God, it was eating the slimy cheese off the slit of my manhood... I felt its' tiny tongue as it ate the caked up grated cheese and my beads of pre cum...

Then, I watched through my tears as my two captors went back up the stairs. I stopped crying and simply looked down and watched as the front of my briefs seemed to bulge and move magically, the mouse's tiny claws torturing my poor cock as it moved around and around in there...

I gasped involuntarily as I felt the creature moving toward my ass cheeks... I quickly squeezed my sexy cheeks together for fear that the thing would try to crawl up and inside me... Good God almighty, just the thought of that was too much to take. The thing made for my butt cheeks, snapping its tiny teeth against them as it ate the cheese all matted up on my sweaty butt cheeks. But then what happened was that the rodent scurried too far downwards and fell out of my briefs from behind. I screamed like a woman as the thing scurried across the floor and out of my sight under the cabinet in which it had been kept in the metal box...

I did my best to regain my sanity and take in my situation...

My muscular body strained and was drenched in sweat under the tight and binding ropes. I stunk of a mixture of fear sweat and grated cheese. Fuck, fuck, I had been kidnapped, stripped, raped and beaten. A mouse was made to eat grated cheese out of my under shorts, while I was wearing them no less... And Cleeve and Otis *still* weren't done with me. What would they do with me when they were done with me??? Would they let me go just like that, satisfied that I had endured their tests and grant me back my freedom???

As I finally caught my breath and regained a semblance of my composure I realized dishearteningly that I had to piss. I also realized that I hadn't had a bite to eat all morning. (Except of course for Cleeve's phlegm.) I had left my apartment at almost five AM. They had grabbed me right after that. The ride to the house, wherever it was, took approximately two to two and a half hours. (I remembered to add in the times that they had stopped to feast on my cock and asshole.) Then, after bringing me to the basement they had left me alone for about an hour or so, I think. By my guessed calculations it had to be around ten AM. I was sure that my instructor at the academy was wondering where I was at that moment. I had not missed one day since I had signed up. Man, would he shit a brick if he or any of my buddies saw the fucked up position I was in at that moment. My cock grew piss hard in my cheesy scented briefs and a little while later Cleeve and Otis returned to the basement. Fuck, the next round was coming up bud…

"Looks like the mouse either found its way out or it slithered up Rookie boy's ass hole," Cleeve laughed as the two men approached me.

My heart pounded with dread…

For the next round of torture I found myself lying across Cleeve's lap with my hands now cuffed behind me as he sat on a straight backed chair, paddling my exposed sexy butt cheeks with a round leather paddle. My under shorts were humiliatingly pulled down in back and tucked under the curve of my ass cheeks.

"Ayyyyyrrrrrr!!!" I cried loudly as Cleeve whacked my butt harder and harder with each blow.

"Give it to him good Cleeve!" Otis said encouragingly to Cleeve as he stood by waiting his turn to paddle me.

My feet were pressed firmly on the floor and tightly tied together at the ankles to keep me from moving off Cleeve's lap as he delivered the fatal spanking.

"ARRRRGghhhhh!!!" I roared as Cleeve gleefully whacked my butt over and over and over again.

"Ha, you know Rookie, a good five or six blows with a leather paddle will usually have a guy screaming from the stinging pain," Cleeve said and whacked me harder and harder. "But we're not going to be all that stingy with you, oh no Sir, we're going for the gusto with you Rookie boy!"

"F-fucking bastard!!! Torturer!!" I ranted, sweating and crying like crazy, scared to death to put it plainly.

After what seemed like hundreds of whacks my poor butt cheeks were more than stinging. I could actually feel them twitching with each blow.

"Ohhhhhrrrrrrrr!!! You sick fucking bastards!!!" I cried pitifully as Cleeve pummeled my butt cheeks.

When he stopped he looked up at Otis, grinning maniacally from ear to ear. He handed Otis the paddle and ran the palm of his hand over my very red, very hot and very wounded butt cheeks. (Fuck, I got the feeling that he could have fried an egg on my poor butt cheeks they felt so hot and crimson.) As I lay there across Cleeve's lap heaving for breath and profusely crying at that point I nearly jumped through the ceiling when he stuck a finger deep in my hole and prodded it.

"*Ullllppppppp!!!*" I gasped in a high-pitched tone of voice and nearly flew off Cleeve's lap.

He dug his finger deeper and deeper into my hole, feeling around in there like he was digging for gold or something.

"Fucker," I said, turning my head and looking despondently at Cleeve. "*Get your damned finger out of my hole man!!*"

He and Otis laughed hysterically as he had a grand old time prodding my hole like crazy. When he stopped he ordered me off his lap and to my (tied) feet. I stood up and did my best to balance myself. I looked utterly ridiculous as I tottered around, almost falling flat on my face. My cock was piss hard as a rock and all slimy; hanging again out of the fly opening of my still cheesy scented briefs. Otis then sat down when Cleeve vacated the chair and then I was lying across his lap next, the mindless Otis, my ass a ready target for the leather paddle again. My cock was aching and really piss hard at that point, pressed against Otis' thigh as he rubbed the paddle against my poor butt cheeks. The paddle actually felt cool against my hot cheeks... Then, he raised the paddle and brought it down hard on my already reddened butt cheeks.

"ARRRHHHH!!!" I cried out all over again and Otis whacked my butt cheeks again and again and again and again, harder and harder with each damned blow.

Otis held me tightly around my waist as he continued paddling my poor crimson butt cheeks. I was in total agony as the guy pummeled and pummeled my poor butt harder and harder. Tears of rage and helplessness flowed freely from my eyes.

"RRRRRRRRR!!!! Bastards!!!" I roared.

Finally Otis stopped paddling me and like Cleeve, ran the palm of his hand over my crimson, red and welted butt cheeks.

"Man, we really gave it to him good," Otis said and slid a finger into my hole.

"ULLLPPP!!!!" I yelped again, as this time Otis prodded my hole good, hard and deep. "Fucking perverts!!"

Cleeve and Otis laughed hysterically as I squirmed miserably strewn across Otis' lap, his finger digging deeper and deeper into my hole. I happened to look across the room and saw the baby mouse scurry under another of the cabinets. I gritted my teeth together and railed over the thought of that rodent scurrying around in my underpants, while I was wearing them no less...

"Man oh man, this rookie is driving me nuts Cleeve," Otis said gleefully.

"Yeah, me too man, me too," Cleeve said. "Let's get ready for the next event Otis. "I'm sure Rookie boy is going to hate it."

"Yeah, but we're going to love it," Otis said.

The two men laughed harder and harder as Otis went on prodding my damned stinking hole. I clenched my teeth again and wondered what the hell they had in mind for me next. The answer wasn't all that long in coming...

Later, the three of us were standing outside the big house. Cleeve and Otis were fully dressed in hiking gear. I was scantily dressed, wearing just my shoes and knee length black socks. Before leaving the house the bastards had stripped me of my uniform shirt and briefs. I felt really vulnerable and very sexy standing there between the two men with all I had hanging out for their perverse pleasures and to do with what they pleased. With my hands not cuffed they held me tightly by my upper muscular arms and walked me into the woods.

"Fuckers!!!" I ranted through clenched teeth. "Where the hell are you guys takin' me now???"

As I struggled in their vise like grasps they hoisted me off the ground and half carried me half dragged me into the woods. In the woods they stopped walking and put me down, still holding tightly onto my arms.

"Ready for a long walk in the woods Rookie boy?" Cleeve asked me, leaned down and stole a hard slurp on one of my sore nipples.

"Unnnghhhhh!!!" I moaned miserably. "What walk in the woods??? I'm not properly dressed for a damn walk in the woods!! Fuck, I'm not properly dressed for shit!!"

"No you're not Rookie boy," Cleeve said and gave my balls a mean tug. "But you're going for a walk anyway. You won't be the first poor fuck that we romped through the woods practically naked. Just another handsome muscle fuck to put to the test..."

Cleeve then noticed a big, long, heavy looking fallen tree branch on the ground and smiled wickedly at me. It was the smile I had come to learn to dread.

"Otis, I have an idea which will make our walk a little easier, for you and I that is," Cleeve said.

The two men let go of my arms and before I could even think to do anything Cleeve kneed me good and hard and awfully in the nuts.

"OHHHHHHHRRRRRR geez man!!!" I grunted madly and loudly, cupping my poor wounded balls in my hands. "FUCK, but that was an crappy thing to do to me…"

As I stood there writhing and moaning in agony the two men picked up the fallen tree branch and laid it across my bare shoulders.

"HOOOFFFFFFFF!!!" I gasped at the weight of the thing and bent over slightly to support it up there on my wide shoulders. *"Wh-what the fuck?"*

They then lifted my wrists against the ends of the thing and tied them up to it, good and tight and secure…

"Ohhhhhhhrrrr shhhiiiit, you bastards!!" I yelled, (my balls still smarting from the blow they'd been dealt) as they tied the tree branch over my shoulders.

The rough bark bit meanly into my skin and the weight of the damn thing was enormous on my shoulders. Once my wrists were securely tied to the tree branch Cleeve suggested that he and Otis hang their heavy and burdensome backpacks on the ends of the branch, making it even heavier for me. I was sweating already and it felt like I was going to fall flat on my face.

"Okay Rookie boy, lets get moving," Cleeve said and squeezed my piss hard cock. "You get to lead the way."

With the heavy tree branch lashed to my shoulders I began walking ahead of my two captors. As I walked slowly and miserably in the heat they threw pebbles at my naked and reddened butt…

"Move it Rookie boy!!" Cleeve yelled harshly and flung a big pebble against my ass.

"OWWWrrrr!!!" I roared.

"We're just getting started on our nature hike!" Cleeve admonished me.

"Th-this tree branch is too fucking heavy!!" I cried pitifully, slightly bent over as I walked, looking miserably from side to side at my wrists tied up to the damned thing as it weighed me down.

"Just walk!!" Cleeve yelled behind me.

Their backpacks swung back and forth on the ends of the tree branch as I plodded on in agony. A few times I stepped in squishy and smelly mud puddles, animal dung I thought a few times as well, getting my police shoes filthy. As we walked through thorn bushes I was pinched and prodded on all parts of my exposed muscular body. I dreaded poison ivy. Sweat was dripping off me everywhere and insects were finding their way to me. Flies landed on my chest and mosquitoes feasted heartily on me. I thought miserably again of the mouse crawling through my underpants while I had been wearing them. Around my crotch area insects were feasting on the dried up grated cheese that was still matted to me. I didn't want to look down when I felt insects crawling on my cock shaft. It's a shitty thing to do a police rookie; a guy who wants to make a better difference in the world, what Cleeve and Otis were doing to me let me tell you...

"RRRRRRR!!!!" I roared through clenched teeth again as the flies landed on my face and crawled on it, nipped at it, making me itch like crazy. "You fucking sick bastards will pay for this, *for all of it!!!*"

As I walked Cleeve stepped up beside me, took a riding crop out of his backpack and whacked my ass hard with it.

"ARRRGHHHHH!!!" I cried loudly.

"Just walk Rookie boy," Cleeve said harshly and whacked my ass again and again, harder and harder to get me moving faster. "Never mind the revenge talk."

After we had been walking for about a half-hour or so Cleeve told me (ordered me) to stop. I did as he said and slowly turned to face him and Otis.

"Man, he looks awful," Otis said mockingly and slapped one of my pecs good and hard.

"Uhhhhhh!!!" I moaned miserably and tottered on my shaky feet.

"Kneel down Rookie boy," Cleeve said to me.

I took a deep a breath and slowly slid to my knees in front of the two men, not really having any choice in the matter. I thought for sure that this was where they were going to kill me. Instead, they stepped close to me and took their giant cocks out of the fly openings in their hiking pants. Again, with no other choice than to do as I was told I sucked their cocks alternately, the two of them sliding their monster cocks in and out of my mouth. I had never sucked a man's cock before, didn't have any lessons in the art of it, but at the moment I was getting a firsthand lesson at it. The tree branch felt like it weighed hundreds and hundreds of pounds at that point as it pressed and weighed down on my now more than aching shoulders. As I sucked Cleeve's giant man meat he held me tightly by the back of my head and pumped it in and out of my mouth savagely.

"Ohhhhhhh yeah, suck my cock you hotter than hot looking rookie boy," Cleeve groaned in ecstasy.

As I sucked and sucked Cleeve's cock Otis rubbed his hard fat cock against my face, stroking it at the same time. Then, Cleeve slid his hardness out of my mouth and before I could take a breath Otis shoved his cock into my mouth again. Feeling like some cheap and overused whore I sucked the guy like crazy as Cleeve stood there stroking his big oversized dong. After a while Otis slid his cock out of my mouth and Cleeve shoved his back in, forcing it down my throat this time. Amazingly I didn't choke or gag. It looked like I was a fast learner. (Hardy har har…) It went on and on like that for quite a while. I don't think they were delighting so much in having their cocks sucked per say; they had each other for that after all. I think it was more that they were enjoying seeing me kneeling there and suffering with that heavy tree branch lashed across my shoulders and weighing down on me. I also think that it was more than giving them their jollies to be making a macho police rookie suck cock.

They shot their pent-up and thick loads together, stroking themselves all over my big muscular chest…

"Ohhhhrrrrrrr yeahhhhhh, yeahhhhhh, fucking A," the two men grunted as they unloaded and came all over my torso.

Their cum was warm and dripped all over my chest, making a real sexy mess as it dripped liberally over my sore nipples and down to my stomach area. As it dripped over my nipples I felt a slight burning sensation, seeing as my poor nubs were all raw and sore from the workout and beatings they'd endured. I couldn't help watching it bud, as their cum sluiced over me. Fuck, they bathed my entire upper body in their thick creamy juices let me tell you. When they were done they packed their giant meat sticks back into their hiking pants and took a hearty gulp of water from their canteens, which were hanging on their supply belts.

"Thirsty Rookie boy?" Cleeve asked me, leering at me.

Thirsty? *Thirsty???* I was fucking drier than a desert. *Yeah, I was thirsty.*

"Y-yeah I am," I replied, looking up at Cleeve beseechingly.

He put his canteen to my trembling lips and I wrapped them snugly around the tip of it. I sipped the cool water slowly. It was delicious. Otis looked at me lustfully as I sipped the water, my lips wrapped seductively around the tip of Cleeve's canteen. When I had drunk enough Cleeve hooked his canteen back onto his belt.

"Okay Rookie boy, *back on your feet!*" Cleeve said to me with total authority.

A look of utter and total defeat crossed over my face and I slowly pulled myself to my aching feet. The tree branch seemed to be pressing down harder than before on my poor shoulders. When I was standing the two men looked me over appraisingly. Their cum was mixed with my sweat all over my massive chest and flat stomach, my chest and butt cheeks and arms were still red and striped from the beatings I had been given and my nipples were still looking more than pretty sore. My shoulders and legs were aching more than miserably and *again* insects were already finding their way to me. Oh yeah, Cleeve and his mindless pal Otis were making sure that I was one very beat to shit rookie cop...

"Otis my man, I just came up with *another great fucking idea,* " Cleeve said, looking wickedly at my sweaty and low hanging balls.

"Ohhhhh no man, *what now???* " I asked dejectedly as Cleeve took some rope out of his backpack, which was still hanging on one end of the tree branch across my shoulders.

Before making me plod on through the woods with that damned tree branch lashed across my aching shoulders Cleeve tied some rope tightly around my balls, not being all that gentle about it either let me mention. As he tied the rope around my family jewels the sleazy dude sniffed at them bud, oh God!! From the look of the grimace on Cleeve's face I guessed that my low hangers smelled pretty bad. Then, Cleeve stepped behind me and told me to get moving again. As I walked Cleeve used the rope as a sort of leash to pull on my balls. The two men laughed hysterically as I walked like a dog on that goddamned leash. My balls were pulled painfully behind me and a few times I thought that Cleeve was going to yank them right off me as he pulled on that damned rope. *What a fucked up situation I was in!!* My cock pointed outwards long and hard in front of me, filled to the boiling point with piss. I didn't dare piss however for fear of what the two men would do to me if I did. Although I didn't see what the big deal would have been if I pissed in the woods. I walked on and on, aching, sweating, gasping for breath and crying silently but profusely. What had I ever done to deserve all this that I had to earn back my freedom I asked myself miserably as I trudged on and on and on…

"Enjoying the walk Otis?" Cleeve asked.

"Sure am Cleeve," Otis responded. "I just love being one with nature every once in a while."

"What about you Rookie boy?" Cleeve asked and yanked on the rope around my balls. "Are you enjoying the walk so far?"

"Yeah, *it's just fucking great!!* " I replied breathlessly and sarcastically, snot now dripping from my nose and onto my lips as I spoke. "Just what I've always wanted to do."

The two men laughed again, Cleeve pulled hard on the rope and I screamed out loudly and in pain. Birds flew recklessly out of trees at the sound of my loud scream. A couple of birds must have been really scared because some bird dung plopped down onto my chest. I rolled my eyes in disbelief.

"H-hey guys, *I have to piss!!*" I yelled desperately. "How about it huh? I have to piss real fucking bad!"

"We'll consider that request soon Rookie boy," Cleeve replied and gave my balls another tug. "In the meantime just keep on walking."

I looked down at my feet and again did as I was told. My police issue patent leather lace-up shoes were by then covered in mud and dirt. My black dress socks were more than spotted with mud and dirt and dung as well. Flies and other summer insects were crawling over my knees. They also crawled on my thighs and the backs of my thighs, making me itch like crazy. I felt insects crawling over my ass cheeks and when I looked down there was a big bumblebee crawling through the sweat, cum and bird dung all over my chest. It stopped on one of my nipples, of all places and I thought that for sure it was going to sting me. But after sitting there on my sore nipple for a few long minutes it flew off. I cried harder and harder, sniveling in agony and humiliation. I mean, *fuck,* how often does a guy have a bee land on one of his damned tits? As my tears flowed down my cheeks I plodded on miserably, (more than miserably actually) my balls aching under my ass crack, that was how far Cleeve had yanked them back at that point. Then, at one awful point I felt what I was sure were big old horse flies crawling over my ass crack. I feared that they would find their way into my asshole, just like the mouse earlier so I squeezed my sexy butt cheeks together as tightly as possible as I plodded on and on. Cleeve and Otis saw what I was doing and laughed hysterically and mockingly.

"I just love seeing him suffer," Cleeve said jokingly.

"Me too Cleeve," Otis agreed stupidly and threw a few pebbles real hard at my butt cheeks.

Even though it hurt and stung like the devil I kept my ass cheeks squeezed tightly together, my crack closed, still fearing that the flies I felt back there would somehow get inside my hole. God!!! When Otis threw more pebbles at my butt cheeks the flies flew off.

"Halt Rookie boy!!" Cleeve then barked at me fifteen or twenty minutes later.

I stopped walking and did my best to stand in place as Cleeve and Otis stepped in front of me. I was heaving for breath by now and they saw that. I was literally sopped in sweat from head to toe and shaking and trembling all over and they saw that too.

"Okay Otis, lets get that tree branch off him," Cleeve said. "We don't want him dropping dead after all."

I was utterly grateful as they untied my wrists from the tree branch, lifted it off my shoulders, took their backpacks off it and chucked it away. I lowered my aching arms to my sides and involuntarily fell to my knees in front of the two men. With my head hanging down I sobbed loud like a man and real miserably.

"B-bastards, *fucking bastards!!!!*" I wailed, shooing insects off me. "Wh-wh-what the fuck are you doin' all this to me for????"

I knelt there more than shaking, crying and needing to piss like never before in my young life. I then looked up at my captors but saw no mercy whatsoever in their eyes.

"On your feet Rookie boy," Cleeve said, giving my balls a good hard yank, reminding me of who was in charge.

I found myself a few minutes later tied up with my wrists over me to a tree branch, my feet firmly on the ground and pushed widely apart by an ankle bar hooked up to my socked feet. The ankle bar had been stored in Otis' backpack. When he took it out it was actually three rods that fitted together to make one long ankle bar. My asshole was totally exposed for their perverse pleasures. I could not move as they squatted behind me sticking their fingers into my hole, licking and sucking at it as well.

"ARRRHHHHHHH!!!!" I cried loudly as they feasted meanly on my mangy hole.

My balls were still tied and in between lapping my hole Cleeve would give them a good hard yank, getting a good scream out of me each time.

"Man oh man, his hole looks ready," Otis said eagerly.

"Sure does Otis my man," Cleeve said. "And seeing as he was your find I'll let you go first."

"Go first for what?" I asked, fearing what I already knew. "What the hell are you goin' to do to me now?"

The two men stood up. Otis was behind me and Cleeve was in front. As Cleeve squeezed my nipples I felt it, Otis' cock was nibbling at my open and stretched asshole.

"Ohhhhhhhrrrrrr no, *no!!! Ohhhrrrr you bastards, not this!!!*" I cried out loudly as Otis' fat cock slowly entered me. "Ohhhhhhrrr you fucking bastards, *you lowlifes!!*"

I again clenched my teeth and balled my roped hands into fists in total agony as Otis' cock slid deeper into me. It felt as if I was being wedged open more and more back there as he entered my most private space.

"Urrrrrrggghhhhhh!!!! No, please man, *no!!!*" I begged as Cleeve continued squeezing and twisting my nipples hard, looking at me lecherously.

Then, Otis pushed hard and his big cock was all the way inside me. I screamed in wretched pain as my asshole lost its virginity.

"OHHHHHHHHHHH no!!!!" I cried as Otis' cock painfully filled my hole, spearing me.

I bucked my muscular body back and forth as Otis pumped his manhood in and out of my hole, harder and harder with each blasted thrust. As Otis fucked me like crazy I watched as Cleeve let go of my sore nipples, slid to his knees in front of me and greedily slurped my piss hard cock into his mouth. He began sucking me ferociously as Otis fucked me and fucked me, running his big mangy hands all over my chest, squeezing my nipples and caressing me like crazy.

"Ohhhhhhrrrrr God," I whispered breathlessly as my head spun. *"Fuckers are driving me batty!!"*

Otis pumped in and out of my hole faster and faster and still faster, his strong arms wrapped snugly around my torso, mashing my hole to mince meat it felt like. Then, he panted in my ear that he was cumming, licking and slurping at my earlobe at the same time, drooling.

"Ohhhhh yeahhhh, you fucking hot rookie boy," Otis panted, drooling liberally in my ear, his cock wedged deep in my hole.

I felt his warm juices flood my hole as he exploded deep inside me, holding me tighter and tighter against him, shuddering, as he seemed to cum and cum.

"Ohhhhhh yeahhhh yeahhhhhh!!!" Otis bellowed as he came and came in gushes.

Suddenly, unbelievably, I felt myself cumming as well, right into Cleeve's mouth. He sucked me more than ferociously, gulping down my jizz like an animal in heat.

"ooooooooohhhhh!!!" I panted, feeling dizzy and totally disoriented.

Cleeve let my cock slip out of his mouth as Otis slowly pulled his cock out of my asshole. I stood there totally breathless as Cleeve stroked my super sensitive, slimy and sexy cock, causing me to piss and piss and piss all over my mud, dung and dirt covered police issue shoes. My piss washed away some of the dirt and mud and crap that was all over my shoes, revealing some of the patent leather shine again. But fuck it all man, that's an awful thing for a cop, or even a rookie cop to behold, to see himself, or even someone else pissing on his police issue shoes. It sort of said something about my entire fucked up situation, revealing how it was Cleeve and Otis who had me under their total control, up to and including making me piss, and on my damned shoes no less.

"AHHHHHHHHHH!!!! Making me piss my damned guts out!!" I roared as Cleeve held my manhood tightly in his hand, squeezing my yellow stream from it, it seemed.

God, it almost felt as good as when I had pissed in the shower that morning. The scent of my piss wafted up to my nose and the scent of it made my cock get hard again. Cleeve smiled mockingly at me. Actually it was a knowing smile that he was sporting as my cock grew stiff yet again. When I was (finally) done pissing Cleeve let go of my cock and hurried behind me. He pressed the crown of his giant (much bigger than Otis') cock against my sopping wet and twitching asshole.

"Ohhhhhhhhh no, no, not you too Fucker!!" I moaned and groaned miserably as Cleeve's cock entered me, inch by painful inch.

When Cleeve plunged his giant meat stick into my poor hole I felt my crevice being stretched beyond its limits. My head was spinning out of orbit as Cleeve rammed my hole far worse than Otis had done. Otis stood in front of me squeezing, teasing and tweaking my nipples, twisting them hard as Cleeve meanly pummeled my hole with his big cock.

"Fucking bastards!!" I seethed as they worked me like crazy.

Cleeve fucked me longer than Otis had and harder as well. When he shot his load he shot a load bigger than Otis' had been. He held me so fucking tight against himself that I thought I would suffocate to death right there man.

"Ohhhhhhhrrrrr shiiiittttt, yeahhhhh oh yeah, fucking A Rookie boy!!" Cleeve roared as he shot his pent-up juices into me, thrusting hard at the same time.

Finally, his giant cock slid out of my hole and he and Otis sat down on the ground at my ankle barred feet to relax.

"Whooooooo, that was fucking great," Cleeve grunted happily.

"Sure as shit was," Otis said. "Nothing like a good hard fuck in the woods in a tight hole."

"Best rookie boy I've seen in a long fuckin' time," Cleeve said and ran his hand gingerly over one of my long black socks. "Fucking hottest rookie boy we've had in a long time."

He snapped the elastic in my sock against my leg and he and Otis kissed each other on the lips, hard and passionately. A while later they took the ankle bar off my feet and untied my wrists from the tree branch and with the rope still wound around my poor aching balls they sat me on a nearby tree stump with my hands now tied securely at the wrists in front of me and my feet tied together. Cleeve and Otis sat on the ground a few feet from me while we all ate sandwiches which they had had in their backpacks and drank water from their canteens. I gulped down a plain bologna sandwich followed quickly by another and then another I was that hungry. And just for the record I never eat cold cuts.

"Eat up Rookie boy," Cleeve said and handed me another sandwich. "You must be more than fucking ravenous after the workout we just gave you."

"Why are you doin' this to me?" I asked them for what seemed like the hundredth time.

The two men looked at each other and then back at me, seeming to drink in the sight of me sitting there naked except for my shoes and socks out in the woods.

"I guess because we chose you Rookie boy," Cleeve said. "You are our most recent choice."

"Y-you mean to say that you've done this sort of thing to other men before me?" I asked them in disbelief, and still hungry took a bight of my fifth sandwich.

"We sure have Rookie boy," Cleeve replied and took a hearty gulp of his water.

"Wh-where are those men now?" I asked them, fearing the answer I would hear.

"Back where we found them I would suppose," Cleeve said. "We never killed anybody and we always release our conquests when we're done with them, some a little later than others but we always release them. One of them, well, we'll release him someday…"

The two men again looked at each other, grinned and laughed hysterically.

"What the fuck is so funny?" I asked them. "Kidnapping is a federal offense and…"

But before I could finish my sentence Cleeve grabbed the slack of the rope around my balls and gave it a hard tug.

"Uhhhhhhhh!!!!" I moaned in the sudden pain and jumped to my bound feet.

I stood there in agony as Cleeve and Otis took turns tugging on the rope, torturing the bejesus out of my poor balls. They laughed loudly and hysterically as I hopped around stupidly on my tied up feet, my sandwich held tightly in one of my tied hands. They went on and on tugging on that rope, making me dance as they laughed and laughed…

When we were all done with our lunches my balls were pretty swollen and aching horribly. Cleeve had untied my feet and him and Otis packed the sandwich wrappers back into their backpacks as I stood nearby with my hands now tied securely behind me, my shoulders hunched up. Flies and mosquitoes were again crawling all over my chest and I saw an insect that I could not identify crawling its way up one of my socks.

"Shit…" I muttered and shook my leg vigorously, making the insect fly off.

"Hey Otis, I have something in my backpack that will really make this walk miserable for him," Cleeve said, reaching into his backpack and bringing out a long, fat and pink butt plug. "Hey Rookie boy, ever had that hot hole of yours plugged before?"

Smiling, Cleeve held up the butt plug. I gulped hard as he and Otis walked over to me. Even though my feet were untied there was no escape. Even if

I tried to run for it all Cleeve had to do was yank on that rope tied around my poor balls. That would have me stopped more than quickly in my tracks let me tell you bud. And with my hands roped up behind me I didn't stand a chance out there by myself against the elements. The two men slumped me over the tree stump that I had been sitting on while we had eaten, pulled my legs far apart exposing my asshole (again) and slowly forced the butt plug inside me.

"Ohhhhhhrrrrrr shiiittttt!!!" I rasped as Otis did the honors of holding my butt cheeks apart and Cleeve did the other honors of slowly pushing the damned thing into me, further with each thrust.

The bark of the tree stump irritated my chest and the tips of my shoes were pressed into the mushy dirt. Finally, the damn butt plug was all the way in my hole. Otis let go of my ass cheeks and they closed around the invasive thing. I felt like a stopped up drain as Cleeve pulled me to my feet.

"Okay Rookie boy, lets get moving again," Cleeve said and yanked on the rope *still* tied around my balls.

I grimaced in pain and began walking ahead of my two captors...

"I'm glad we brought along some toys that we can use on him out here," Cleeve said to Otis.

"Yeah, me too," Otis agreed. "That was good thinking on your part Cleeve."

"Wait till he sees what else we've got in our backpacks to use on him," Cleeve said fiendishly.

"When do you want to start heading back to the house?" Otis asked.

"Not for a while yet," Cleeve replied. "It's still early so we have plenty of hours of daylight left, *and plenty of time to keep working over our hot and sweaty rookie boy.* Get a move on Rookie boy!!!"

Cleeve gave the rope a good hard tug and I plodded on faster, grunting miserably as I walked. The butt plug felt awful in my hole and tormented me like crazy as I walked on. Fuck, for whatever the reason having that plug wedged tight in my hole made me feel like I had to shit my guts out, but of course with that thing in me that was impossible. What a fucked up feeling bud. The only good thing about that butt plug being wedged up in my hole was that the flies and mosquitoes couldn't get in there if they wanted to now. *And* I wouldn't have to squeeze my butt cheeks together again…

A few minutes or so later I noticed that the strange looking insect that I had shaken off my sock earlier was back for a second trip up my muscular leg. As I walked I saw it land on my long sock and begin moving slowly up my leg. No doubt I still smelled of grated cheese around my crotch area and that bug was intent on getting a taste of it. God!! I realized that it was a big stinging wasp. I feared that it was poisonous and that it would sting me on the leg, thus making it more than difficult for me to walk. I didn't see Cleeve and Otis heaping any sympathy on me if I were stung and not able to move as fast as they would want me to. When I stopped walking to try to shake it off again Cleeve gave the rope around my balls a hard tug to get me moving.

"ARRRGGGHHH!!!" I wailed as my poor nuts were horribly yanked. (I wondered just how much more my poor family jewels could take being tied up and yanked on like they were.) "H-hey guys, listen up, *please!!* Th-there's a damned wasp on one of my socks!! Fucking thing is crawling up my leg!!"

In response Cleeve and Otis simply laughed. The thing slithered slowly up my leg sending squirming like chills through me. When it was on my thigh I started sweating even more, in total fear. Flies and mosquitoes were all over my massive chest and back and crawling over my sweat sopped face. The wasp crawled up toward my pubic bush of hair. Yep, I was right bud, it smelled the grated cheese matted to my crotch and wanted a sampling of it. As it moved more and more squirming chills went through me and sick feeling goose bumps broke out all over me.

"G-guys please, *it's headed for my cock!!*" I cried out.

Otis came running up next to me and shooed the wasp off me.

"Th-thank you," I gasped and he gave me a hard slap on the ass.

But even though the wasp was gone the mosquitoes and flies were still all over me, biting me, feasting on me. I could actually feel them biting me on the chest, my thighs, and my legs and even on my face. We stopped walking again about a half-hour or so later. By then I was looking a lot worse than I had earlier. My short hair was drenched in sweat and matted to my head. Sweat dripped off me everywhere and I sat there in the dirt on my knees catching my breath as my two captors' guzzled water from their canteens.

"Mmmmmm, ahhhhhh!!" Cleeve sighed as he drank water. "You thirsty Rookie boy?"

"Y-yeah, I'm thirsty," I whispered miserably, looking up at Cleeve despondently.

"Say yes Sir I'm thirsty and I'll consider giving you a drink," Cleeve said to me sternly. "I'm just a tad sick and fucking tired of your attitude Rookie."

I looked up at him blankly, not believing what he had just said. It did however give me a small clue as to who Cleeve was.

"Y-you bastard," I said through clenched teeth. "Made me into your damned whipping boy!"

I took a deep breath, swallowed my pride and spoke.

"Sir, I am really thirsty, *Sir!!*" I barked out loud as I knelt there with my poor balls and hands tied and my butt plugged. "Sir, may I have a drink *Sir?*"

Cleeve and Otis looked at each other and smiled with total and sick satisfaction. Then, Cleeve reached down and put the canteen to my trembling lips. I drank the water greedily. Fuck, but *I was thirsty.* When Cleeve felt that I had drank enough he pulled the canteen away from my mouth.

"That's enough Rookie boy, now thank me good and proper," Cleeve said as he capped his canteen.

"Th-thank you Sir," I gasped and leaned down to kiss the tops of Cleeve's hiking boots.

"Looks like we've trained him real well Cleeve," Otis said.

"We sure did," Cleeve said, looking down at me lustfully. "Otis my man, get some rope out of your backpack."

I looked up and gulped again, realizing that I was now in for more nastiness. Moments later I was tied securely to another large tree, as Cleeve and Otis squatted in front of me, licking, lapping and sucking heartily on my aching, sweaty and stinking and still bound up balls.

"Ayyyyyyrrrrrrrr!!!!" I screamed in a man's agony as the two men happily tortured my mangy nuts. "Ohhhhhhrrrrr you blasted fuckers!!"

I writhed in total misery under the tight binding ropes, my muscles flexing everywhere, straining, as my cock grew long, beefy and hard. What was up with that shit anyway? Was what these two bastards were doing to me somehow arousing the fuck out of me? Jeez, I would have a lot to think about if I lived through this let me tell you man. Together, they sucked my balls into their mouths, pressed their tongues against them and applied God-awful pressure to them.

"AYYYYYYYRRRR!!!!" I screeched and my voice echoed mightily through the dense woods.

When the two men stopped feasting on my nuts my poor family jewels were swollen even more and aching worse from being bound for so damned long. Otis had the privilege of jacking me off. He stroked my stiff cock fast, hard and meanly, making me shoot a painful load of rookie cop jizz onto my filthy shoes.

"ACCCHHHHHHH!!!!" I sputtered as I shot my load in pain.

What a twist, shooting a load is supposed to feel great and joyous for a guy. Instead I was feeling miserable and in total agony as I came again for my two captors. Fuckers, they played me like I was a musical instrument of some kind, knowing which strings to strum to get me all melodious and crooning. When I was done grunting and shooting my load the butt plug tormented the fuck out of my hole ten times more. It would seem that, like most men, after shooting a load (or a few) most parts of my body became super sensitive. And at that moment my poor asshole was beyond sensitive bud.

"Fucking bastards," I whimpered as they untied me from the tree, leaving my hands tightly secured behind me.

"Okay Rookie boy, it's time to make those police issue shoes of yours into a pair of dancing shoes," Cleeve then said, opening the zipper on a big section of his backpack. "Otis, if you would be so kind as to "grease" up our rookie boy…"

That said Cleeve reached into his backpack and brought out a large jar of honey and a basting brush. My cock twitched all slimy and soft and long between my muscular legs…

A few seconds later I was standing with my legs slightly parted as Otis squatted beside me and did as Cleeve had instructed him, namely he was "greasing" me, slathering a goodly amount of the honey all over my big beefy cock with the basting brush. Every time the honey smeared basting brush slid over my sore slimy cock it got a good breathless sounding grunt out of me.

"F-fuckers, wh-what're you goin' to do with my cock?" I asked miserably when Otis was done.

And when he was done I was (unbelievably) semi stiff and somewhat hard as a rock, my bound aching balls all swollen and hanging down real low. My cock hung semi hard between my legs actually, pointing straight down at the ground, just the way my captors wanted it. My honey-smeared manhood smelled real sweet and glistened in the sun. Then, my chin dropped a few inches as my mouth fell open in shock when I saw the next item that that monster Cleeve took out of his backpack. I stood there sweating in my socks as he held up a clear plastic quart sized bottle. The bottle had a wine cork squeezed into its top, the wine cork had tiny air holes cut into it. My eyes opened wide in horror as I saw the nearly one hundred or more mosquitoes and flies buzzing around in the bottle.

"Ohhhhhh no, no, *not what I'm thinking you're thinking you sick fucks,"* I grumbled under my breath as the two men laughed sadistically.

I was rooted to the spot in horror as Cleeve took the cork out of the bottle, put his hand over the top so that the occupants stayed within and he and Otis stepped over to me…

"Ohhhhhhhrrrr God no, no!!!!!" I screamed and wailed as Otis held me balanced by my upper arms and Cleeve did the honors of sliding my honey-slicked cock into the neck of the bottle. "OHHHHHRRRRR you fuckers, you sick twisted bastards!!!"

As my thick cock slid into the bottle it seemed to harden just a tad more and when Cleeve let go of it the thing hung off my cock like some sick decoration on a perverted Christmas tree…

I threw my head back and jiggled my cock back and forth in the hopes of getting the insect filled bottle off my manhood before those blasted mosquitoes and flies picked up the scent of my honey smeared cock.

"Ohhhhhhhrrrrr no, no, *no!!!!!*" I wailed; doing a stupid dance in my police issued shoes, just as Cleeve had said that I would. "Get it off me you bastards, *oh god, get it off!!!!*"

But then, as I knew they would the mosquitoes and flies in the bottle picked up on the scent of the honey all over my poor cock. Standing behind me Cleeve yanked on the rope around my balls, getting me dancing some more… It wasn't long before I had a lot more than a few mosquitoes and flies clinging to my shaft, the tip of my cock and crawling along all over it as they ate the honey. Insects are totally and incredibly drawn to the scent of honey, just in case you didn't know that bud… The feeling of the insects as they crawled on my manhood ate the honey and nipped at me was maddening to say the least. With my broad shoulders hunched up and my wrists straining mightily in the bonds I screeched, screamed and jumped up and down and all around, dancing stupidly as the insects in the bottle feasted on my cock like it was a buffet.

"Get it off me you mugs, *ohhhhh God, get it off me!!!*" I begged loudly.

I slammed my ripped muscular back up against a tree, the one I had been tied to actually and swung my bottle covered cock from side to side in the hopes of having it fall off my cock… But I had no luck in that area as the thing hung on my cock. And woe of woes my cock just seemed to get harder and harder, thus embedding it in the insect filled bottle tighter and tighter…

Cleeve yanked hard on the rope tied around my balls, getting a good shrill sounding "OOOOOOO" out of me, my mouth shaped into an "O" and I trudged awkwardly away from the tree I was leaned up against. Once again I was screaming and jumping up and down, the sight totally awful in the bottle, the sight of my cock as more and more flies and mosquitoes found their way from the bottom of it and to the feast of honey on my manhood. I even tried swinging my cock back and forth and slamming the bottle against the tree in the hopes of having it break. But the damned thing was plastic after all…

All I succeeded in doing was hurting my poor cock some more… As I watched a big old horsefly slither across the slit of my cock I thought for sure that I would go totally insane. The itching feeling was immense… With my head spinning I flopped to my knees in the dirt and with my head hanging down I cried and heaved…

A little while later Otis held me balanced again by my upper arms as Cleeve slowly (carefully?) slid the bottle off my cock…

"Th-thank you, thank you, *oh God thank you man,*" I blubbered as some of the flies and mosquitoes flew off while others remained in the bottle.

The insects that were still on my cock Cleeve shooed away… I stood there gasping, nearly retching…

"F-fucking bastards, sh-shitty thing to do to a New York Police rookie," I garbled under my breath, looking down and seeing the tiny bite marks on my honey-slicked manhood. "Real shitty…"

"How many miles do you suppose we've walked?" Otis asked Cleeve, seeming to ignore my ranting and ravings.

"Not all that many," Cleeve replied. "But I'll bet it feels like hundreds to Rookie boy here."

The two men guffawed loudly and I leaned my head against the tree that I was standing against again. Hearing them constantly laughing at me were worse, I think, than the physical tortures they were dishing out on me. It just made my horrible situation seem that much shoddier bud.

"But, the further we go the further we'll have to walk back," Cleeve said and looked at his watch. "Maybe at this point we should start heading on back."

They both looked at me and they each gave my nipples a quick suck each.

"Ready to head on back Rookie boy?" Cleeve asked me and undid the rope around my balls.

"Yeah, I guess so," I said, heaving a loud sigh of relief.

"Don't be so thankful just yet Rookie boy," Cleeve said, reaching into his backpack again. "Those balls of yours still have some suffering to do."

I shuddered as he rummaged around in that blasted backpack…

He pulled a leather ball separator out of his backpack and I gulped hard.

"Ohhhhhhhh no," I moaned.

As Cleeve snapped the device tightly around my swollen aching balls Otis yanked the butt plug out of my hole. (With that new device now tethered to me my family jewels hung perilously far apart.) I suddenly felt a cool draft invade my hole when the device came out. I farted loud and uncontrollably and the two men laughed heartily. I farted again; a wet and watery one and my two captors erupted into massive fits of laughter.

"Whoooooooo, Rookie boy is stinking up the woods!" Otis laughed, and gave one of my red butt cheeks a good squeeze.

As he squeezed my butt cheek I farted again, on purpose this time, although the perv squeezing my ass didn't need to know that.

"Okay Rookie boy, lets get a move on," Cleeve said, giving my ass a hard slap.

My tied balls dangled low, swollen and unnaturally separated between my legs as I began the long walk back toward the house. I was still sweating profusely and each step I took was murder on my poor testicles as they swung in pain between my aching legs. We walked back basically the same way that we had walked going into the woods. When we walked past the tree branch I had carried across my shoulders I was afraid that one of my captors would suggest lashing it across my shoulders again. But no one said a word and we walked past it without incident. The insects again had a grand old time with me though. I felt them crawling over my ass cheeks, my thighs and my face. I had to squeeze my ass cheeks tightly together again as I walked on in the intense heat and massive humidity. A few flies and mosquitoes found their way to my still honey-smeared cock and feasted on it. I was too tired and my throat too scratchy to scream and garble anymore. After a few seconds being on my cock the insects would fly off, maddening as it felt. When we got back to the house I was more than exhausted. I was literally and more than totally beat to shit. There were insect bights all over my chest, stomach, legs and cock. (I wondered if any of the bights were poisonous.) I was itching like crazy from the bights and I was in pain like I had never known before in my life. My legs and arms were totally scratched up from the thorn bushes I had walked through instead of around. My ass cheeks were all red, welted and beaten looking from the pebbles that Cleeve and Otis had thrown at them. They must have pitched in professional baseball or something, because I have to tell you bud, those pebbles stung like crazy when they slammed against my sexy ass cheeks. It felt as if Cleeve and Otis had been hurling them at better than ninety miles per hour. And of course, not to mention the beatings the two men had administered to my poor ass cheeks. Cleeve took the ball separator off my nuts and gave them a hard mean squeeze, managing to get a loud and high-pitched screech out of me. Now my throat was even scratchier. I almost jumped out of my shoes and socks as the pain coursed through me.

"You ready for your ride home Rookie boy?" Cleeve asked me and squeezed my sore nipples next, giving them a mean twist.

I looked at him in disbelief. Were they really going to let me go???

"You did well out there Rookie boy, a lot better than even some soldier boys or marines have fared," Cleeve said, almost sounding proud of me. "Looks like you've won your freedom back again…"

Again I had this small inkling of knowing just who Cleeve was…

A few minutes later I again found myself hooked up in the back of their van. I was dressed in my police rookie uniform and blindfolded. The rope that had been tied around my balls was finally off me as well, although when whichever of the two men took it off me did so I didn't know who it was, seeing as my eyes had already been covered at that point. I heard the back door of the van roll shut and then we were on our way. My heart pounded in fear nonetheless because I didn't know for sure that they were letting me go. Riding me in the van could just be the prelude to more nastiness. The ride back seemed to take longer than the ride to Cleeve's big house. I was able to smell myself and I didn't like it. I smelled of sweat, cum and a little piss thrown in. My crotch emanated a sickly scent of cheese going sour. My socks felt soggy against my feet and my legs and feet ached miserably. All along the way I swore to myself that I would see Cleeve and Otis in jail for all that they had done to me *and* for all that they had done to the other nameless and faceless men out there who had fallen victim to them. When the van stopped more than a couple of hours later I heard the back door roll open.

"Do it quick!!" I heard Cleeve yell from the driver's seat.

Otis came into the back of the van, released me from my bonds and grabbed my arms in a firm and powerful grip.

"H-hey, *what is this???*" I snarled angrily. "You two think you're going to get away with all this that easily? Well, you both sure as shit got another thing coming! You fuckers are under arrest as of this moment man!!"

As I ranted and raved he moved me toward the open door of the van. I knew this because I could feel a warm breeze on my face.

"Bastard!!" I yelled helplessly. "Get this fucking blindfold off me already!! You two are headed for jail!! Even though I'm just a rookie…"

Then, my words were cut short as Otis literally tossed me out of the van and onto the sidewalk.

"Uhhhhhnnnfffff!!!" I gasped as I hit the pavement flat on my ass.

I heard the van pulling away and I quickly yanked the blindfold off, leaving it dangling loosely around my neck. I was too late to get the license plate number of the van as it sped away. Sitting there on the ground I saw that I was back at the exact spot where Cleeve and Otis had abducted me from earlier that day. Although at that point it seemed so long ago, seeing as I had been put through such horrors. At that time in the late afternoon it was not as deserted, as it was early in the morning when they had so expertly snagged me. What a sight I must have made sitting there on the ground in my scuffed up rookie uniform, looking all beat to shit, smelling like crap, and with a damned blindfold dangling around my neck. Two guys, both of them nineteen or twenty years old or so from the neighborhood came running over to me, looks of concern etched on their faces.

"Hey man, are you okay?" the first one, a blond guy asked me as they looked down at me on the ground.

"I-uh, fuck, *I don't know dudes,*" I replied as I watched the van disappear up the block. "D-did either of you guys happen to get the license plate number of that damned van?"

"No man, sorry," the second guy, a husky dude with brown wavy hair replied. "Say Rookie, what's this all about? We saw you get thrown from the van."

"Yeah, and you were blindfolded," the first guy added, reaching down and tugging on the white cloth hanging around my neck. "Is this part of some rookie initiation for cops like they do to pledges in college fraternities?"

"I wish it were, those two bastards *kidnapped me,*" I replied angrily. "Fuck, kidnapped me and fucking tortured the hell out of me. *Shit, shit!!!! What a fucked up thing to do to a rookie police officer!!*"

The two guys helped me to my feet. I looked around and by some stroke of strange luck saw my big book bag on the corner of the street.

"I do not fucking believe it," I said, walked over to the bag on wobbly feet, picked it up and stood there still looking up the block.

I could no longer see the van.

"Fucking kidnappers," I said through clenched teeth.

"You need some help getting home Rookie?" the second guy asked me, looking real concerned. "You don't look like you're in such good shape to even walk a block."

"No, I can make it," I said and started walking toward my apartment building.

After just a few steps though my legs gave out and buckled. As I almost hit the pavement again the two guys came running up to me and grabbed my arms. They held me up as my head spun.

"Come on Rookie, we'll help you home," the blond guy said, taking my book bag from me. "Just point us in the right direction.

As we walked I could see them looking across me at each other and wriggling their noses. Obviously I smelled pretty bad…

When we got to my apartment the two guys helped me out of my shirt and tie (I didn't ask them to strip me, they just did it) and looked at my massively muscular chest in awe.

"Shit Rookie, just what the fuck did those guys do to you?" the brown haired guy asked me, running his fingertip over my sore and aching nipples.

"Like I told you, they fucking tortured me," I grunted, choking back tears of humiliation.

The two guys looked across me and at each other.

"Well, hopefully this will help you feel better Rookie," the blond guy said and together they leaned down and gently tongued my nipples into their mouths.

"Ohhhhh yeahhh, it sure does," I whispered. *"It sure as shit does."*

A few years have gone by since that fateful day at the hands of Cleeve and Otis. I am a New York City police officer now and damned fucking proud of it let me tell you bud. I haven't heard anything about them since and I never heard of anyone reporting being kidnapped and tortured by them. But someday, I vow, I will see those two fuckers again. And when I do I will tell them of my Friday night antics at the leather bar that I hang out in.

And I'll even tell them about my lust for pain and ecstasy at the same time…

THE CONSTRUCTION WORKER

My name is Jimmy. I'm a construction worker with a company called "Green's Construction." I'm six feet two inches tall, I have silky jet black hair, dark, slightly slanted eyes because I am half American and half Asian, and my body is extremely muscular and toned from the work that I do every day. The story I want to tell you happened six months ago. (I have finally gotten up the nerve to tell it…) My crew and I (I'm a construction supervisor as well as a worker) had been hired by a Real Estate agency to redo the fifth floor of their building. We worked late that Monday to get everything going. We had only two weeks to get the entire job done. Actually, that was more than enough time for my crew and me. At seven o'clock that night I sent all the guys home. They were tired from working hard all day ripping the fifth floor apart since eight o'clock that morning. I lagged behind in what was left of one of the offices to look over the blueprints for how the floor would look when we were done and also to look over some of the accounting paperwork. Sitting at the desk I decided I wanted a soda. I went down to the lobby where there was a soda machine to get a can of Pepsi. What I didn't know was that two prowlers were hiding in the fire stairwell of the building, going from floor to floor, ripping off office equipment and whatever safes they could bust into. When they got to the fifth floor I was in the lobby getting my soda.

"Hey, they're renovating this floor!" the first prowler said. "Let's skip it. What a fucking mess…"

"Nah." his friend disagreed. "Look, there's an office over there. I'll go through the desk and see what goodies I can find while you keep watch at the door."

"Okay." the first prowler replied.

As the second prowler was rummaging through the desk I had vacated a few minutes earlier his friend was standing watch by the door. I came back up with a cold can of Pepsi in my hand, not knowing the kind of night it was about to turn into…

I stepped into the office and saw the second prowler squatting at the desk.

"Hey, who the fuck are you?" I asked him loudly, not knowing his buddy was right behind me.

As I was about to stomp over to him his friend grabbed me from behind by my muscular yet very tired arms.

"H-hey!!!" I gulped, dropping my can of soda, the contents of it spilling on the floor.

"Well, well, looks like we have company." said the prowler who had grabbed me.

And grabbed me tight I might add…the fucker had a grip like steel. I struggled in his grip as his friend walked over to us.

"Who the fuck are you two?" I asked in anger. "How the hell did you get in here???"

The first prowler pushed my arms in front of me so that his friend could grab my wrists and hold them tightly together. I struggled like crazy in their grasps.

"Whoooo!!!" the first prowler whooped happily. "What a great big hunk he is! Fuckin' muscle boy if ever there was one. Hold him tight Otis! We don't want this boy here running off to the police!"

"Gotcha Cleeve!" the second prowler replied and tightened his grip on me.

"Fuckin' crooks!!!" I yelled. "I know who you two are!! You're the guys I read about in the paper who have been ripping off office buildings!"

"How right you are big guy!" Otis said, squeezing my arms tighter and tighter. "Hey Cleeve, look! There's some rope on the floor over there. Let's tie this big galoot up and get on with the task at hand."

"No *No!!!!*" I yelled as they forced me (practically hoisting me off the damned floor...strong fuckers they were...) across the room. "Bastards!!! Don't fucking tie me up you guys!!!"

In moments I was tied standing up with my wrists in front of me. My wrists were tightly tied together and roped to a large pile of cinder blocks. They tied my feet securely together and gagged me with a rancid tasting rag from one of their pockets. Cleeve, the bigger of the two men laughed mockingly as he tied a rope tightly over the sweaty and smelly tasting rag crammed in my mouth. I looked at him in utter anger as I struggled to free myself.

"Don't go anywhere now big guy." Cleeve said, patting me on the cheek.

He and Otis went back to ransacking the place as I struggled like crazy to pull free of the ropes.

"Rrrrrmmmmffff!!!" I sputtered angrily.

"Are those ropes on his wrists tied tight enough?" Cleeve asked Otis.

"Sure as shit are." Otis replied. "When I tie a knot it stays tied till I untie it."

"Good..." Cleeve said slowly and lustfully. "Because I want our guy tied up for a while."

I turned my head and saw the two men looking hungrily at my two melon-shaped ass cheeks in my worn blue jeans.

"Otis my man, I'm getting' a real great fucking idea!" Cleeve said, looking at his friend with a fiendish expression on his face.

"Right with you Cleeve." Otis said as they slowly walked over to me.

I turned my head facing forward and gulped loudly behind my gag. In seconds their big hands were all over me, roaming over my blue tee shirt covered chest, my worn blue Levi's jeans covered legs, and even caressing my big bull neck and stealing sucks on my big fingers.

"Ummmmffff!!!!" I reeled at them.

"Rerverts!!!" I sputtered into my gag.

They rolled my tee shirt up over my nipples and each took one of my tits into their mouths, sucking them hard, licking them, even fucking kissing them, and caressing my big muscular pecs at the same time. Otis toyed with my belly button as he nibbled on the tit he had in his mouth. Now, just for the record, I am straight, married, and had never had sex of any kind with a man in my entire life. But now, here I was at the age of thirty- two, being sexually worked over by two horny prowlers. They sucked my nipples till I thought they would bight them off my hairless muscular chest. They slapped my washboard stomach and I felt my dick growing hard in my jeans. Damn!!!

"Hey Otis, lets get our guy undressed and work on his butt!" Cleeve said.

Otis enthusiastically agreed. They abandoned my nipples and with a pair of shears each that they found with my crew's tools they cut my jeans off me. When they got near my crotch area I stood as still as a mannequin, sweating in fear as the shears cut my jeans away. When they were done slicing my jeans off me they cut my tee shirt off me next…the cold metal of the shears rubbed against my skin, sending chills through me…my dick got harder. I was left wearing my white briefs, white sweat socks, and my black, scuffed construction boots.

"RRRRR!!!!" I roared as the two men undressed themselves, my dick hard as a rock in my briefs, pre cum seeping through the cotton material...my dick betraying me.

Then they went back to pawing me. Otis squatted in front of me, took my hard dick out of my white briefs through the fly hole, held it in his hand for a second, squeezed it, and then gobbled it into his mouth and sucked it like crazy.

"MMmmmfff!!!!" I sputtered as my body jerked involuntarily.

As Otis amused himself sucking my big meat Cleeve squatted behind me, pushed the sides of my briefs into the crack of my ass, exposing my melon shaped buns, and began licking and then biting my ass cheeks...hard.

"Urrrrrrr!!!!!" I wailed miserably.

Cleeve didn't just nip at my butt cheeks; he really sank his teeth into them leaving bight marks all over them. Otis ran his hands up and down my legs as he sucked me harder and harder.

"Rastards!!!!!" I yelled into my gag, not believing that I was being sexually worked over by two fucking men.

I struggled like mad to pull free of the damn ropes but it was useless. Cleeve bit harder into my tender ass flesh like he was eating a piece of raw meat. I felt his fingers toying with my thick white sweat socks and the laces on my construction boots. I was infuriated, mortified, and in ecstasy all at the same time. I was going to shoot my load soon if Otis didn't stop sucking my meat. He didn't stop...

"God, his butt is as creamy as a bowl of Cool Whip Otis!!" Cleeve exclaimed. "You have to taste this to believe it!"

"I bet it is!" Otis responded, taking my hard and throbbing dick out of his mouth and holding it tightly in his fist. "His dick ain't too bad tasting either... considering he's probably been sweating like a pig all fucking day."

They resumed their biting of my ass and sucking of my dick. I gyrated my muscular body in what would be thought of as seductive and sexy but actually I was getting closer to shooting a giant load of cum. I felt Otis' tongue teasing the tip of my dick slit and then it was happening. I was cumming.

"MMMfff!!!!" I wailed as I shot my load in Otis' mouth, looking down in utter ecstasy as the bastard sucked me like crazy. "RRRRmmmffff...."

Cleeve bit my ass cheeks harder and harder as I seemed to cum in gushes.

"MMMfffff!!!!" I wailed loudly as saliva dripped out of the sides of my gagged mouth.

Otis swallowed every damn drop of my juices and then took my dick out of his mouth.

"What a load!!!" Otis exulted, looking up at me with total satisfaction, smacking his lips together. "Tasted fucking great too! You must eat a healthy diet big guy!!"

He gave my softening dick a quick lick and stood up, followed by Cleeve. I hung my head down in exhaustion, hoping they would untie me and be on their way. No such luck though. Cleeve and Otis switched places, Otis squatting at my teeth marked butt and Cleeve squatting at my soft dick poking out of my briefs.

"Coming up, round two big guy!" Cleeve said mockingly, slurping my dick into his mouth.

"Ummmmmffff!!!!" I protested, as my dick was still super sensitive from just having shot that first load of nut juice.

Otis ran the palms of his hands over my ass cheeks and licked them heartily.

"Oh Cleeve, what a butt he has at that!!!" Otis said breathlessly, giving one of my ass cheeks a hard squeeze. "I can't wait to get these briefs off him and fuck the crap out of this big guy!!!"

At the sound of those words I reeled like crazy, desperately trying to get free now. *Fuck my ass??? Fuck my ass??? No way!!!! It couldn't happen!!! But unfortunately for me it would happen soon enough...*

Moments past and then I was hard in Cleeve's mouth as he sucked me like crazy. By now I was sweating like crazy and still struggling to pull free of the ropes. Fuck, why oh why did I have to stay late that night?

Otis slapped my ass hard in between taking bights. I felt myself getting close to shooting a second load of cream. Good God almighty, my wife had never been able to get two loads in a row out of me and now these two goddamned rapists were about to. I gyrated myself again as I felt myself getting closer and closer to blast number two.

"Ummmmmmffff..." I said as I began to cum.

Cleeve slapped my thighs as I shot my load into his mouth. His tongue swirled around my dick that was tightly trapped in his mouth and still spewing sperm, driving me crazy...

"MmmmmFFFF!!!" I wailed as he forced more and more cum out of my dick, sucking it like crazy.

Finally, Cleeve took my dick out of his mouth and licked his lips contentedly.

"You do taste great at that big guy!" Cleeve said, giving the tip of my sore dick a pinch.

"RRRmmmfff..." I gasped.

Both men stood up and again ran their hands over my body, caressing my biceps, my chest, my stomach, and my neck. I reeled in the bondage as the two men treated my body like an object...mortified and angry that I could do nothing to stop them. They slurped and sucked my big fingers and even kissed my gagged mouth.

"We're goin' to fuck you now big guy!" Cleeve spat at me. "Is that virgin ass of yours ready for us?"

"MMMFFFF!!!!" I roared at him.

"You really think he has a virgin ass Cleeve?" Otis asked with a hand on my shoulder.

"Yep, positive." Cleeve replied. "This boy is straight as an arrow…"

Cleeve pointed to the wedding band on my left-handed ring finger.

"Whoops, almost missed that." Otis said, slipping my ring off my finger and tossing it with the other stuff they'd stolen.

My eyes filled with tears of anger and anguish because they took the ring that my beautiful and loving wife had placed on my finger the day we were married…and because they were now ripping my briefs off me, preparing me to be fucked.

"Want to take the gag off him for this?" Otis asked. "I'm sure that by now there's no one left in the building to hear him scream when we break that cherry in his butt."

"You read my mind Otis." Cleeve said and took the gag out of my mouth.

"You fucking bastards!!!" I roared at them. *"Perverts!!!! Slime buckets!!! Faggots!!!!!"*

In response to my obscenities Cleeve and Otis just laughed and spit in my face.

"Don't guys, please, *please*, not my ass, don't fuck me!!!!" I begged as I saw them stroking their big, hard, monster sized dicks.

"I go first." Cleeve said anxiously. "Otis, sit in front of our guy, suck his dick, and spread those delectable cheeks of his."

Without a word Otis did as Cleeve asked. He knelt in front of me, gobbled my dick into his mouth, sucked it, and reached around me to grab my ass cheeks with his big fingers. He pulled my cheeks apart, hurting me, and exposing my pink bunghole as Cleeve took his stance behind me.

"God no, don't fucking suck me again man!!!" I yelled down at Otis as he held my ass cheeks painfully apart. "Ohhhhhrrr GOD…"

Then, the worst pain I had ever experienced took me in its grip as Cleeve's dick entered my asshole with no lubricant of any kind.

"Arrrrrr!!!!" I roared in tortured agony.

Cleeve pumped my hole like a crazed madman, thrusting his big dick in and out, slapping my cheeks at the same time.

"Oh yeah yeah!!!" Cleeve roared in wild passion. "What an ass!!! What a tight fuckin' hole!!!"

Otis sucked me till my sore dick was hard…again. He took it in his hand and spun it around painfully as he tugged on my poor balls at the same time.

"Think you can shoot another load big guy?" Otis asked me mockingly and took my dick back in his mouth.

"Arrrghhhh!!!!" I roared. "You fuckers, you blasted perverts!!!"

Cleeve was utterly relentless as he fucked me harder and harder, thrusting deeper and deeper into my poor hole. Then, he pressed himself against my back, wrapped his arms around my upper body, and teased my nipples with his fingers as he held his dick deep inside my hole. I was able to feel it throbbing in there like it had a life of its own. Cleeve nibbled on my ear and whispered breathlessly that he was about to cum.

"Oh God…please…" I moaned.

Then, I felt the heat spewing from Cleeve's dick as he came inside me, filling my hole with his creamy juices.

"Oh yeah!!! Fuckin' A!!!" Cleeve panted as he thrust in me again, hugging me, pinching the fuck out of my nipples, and biting my earlobe.

When he was done his dick slipped out of my hole. He yanked my head back by a handful of my hair and viciously kissed me on the mouth. Otis continued sucking my dick. Tears of anger flowed down my cheeks as Cleeve let go of my hair.

"Your turn Otis." Cleeve said.

"No, oh no, not again!!!" I yelled desperately.

Otis quickly abandoned my dick and stood behind me. Cleeve took Otis' place in front of me, pulled my dick into his mouth, and spread my cheeks apart.

"Man, look at that bunghole of his!!" Otis commented. "It looks good enough to eat."

My eyes rolled in my head as I felt Otis' tongue lapping at my wet hole.

"You bastards!!!" I yelled. "I'll kill you both for this!!! I swear it, if it's the last fucking thing I do I'm going to make you two pay!!!"

I looked down at Cleeve sucking my dick and then I felt myself getting ready to shoot another damned load. (I guess if you suck a guy's dick enough you'll get him off more times than he really wants too...)

"Oh God, you perverts, I'm going to cum again!!!" I shouted.

As I felt myself about to shoot another load Otis' dick entered my ass.

"Arrrghhhh!!!!" I roared as I was fucked a second time and came a third time.

I gyrated my hips as Cleeve swallowed my cum and Otis fucked me mercilessly till he came. He held me by the back of my hair, thrusting in and out of my squishy wet hole.

"Ayyyyrrrr!!!" I screamed in pleasure and in pain at the same time.

I felt Otis' cum fill my hole and then he kissed the back of my big neck as his dick slid out of my hole. I dropped to my knees in exhaustion as the two men caught their breath and began getting themselves dressed.

"Let's get the fuck out of here." Cleeve said. "We got what we came for plus more!"

"We sure did." Otis agreed happily.

I kneeled there heaving, my bound wrists above me. I was sobbing and shaking as they each gave my ass a kick before leaving me there alone. After a while I managed to get a grip on myself, used my teeth to undo the knots in the ropes on my wrists, pulled myself to a sitting position against the pile of cinder blocks, and untied my feet. I ran my hand through my sweat drenched hair, looked down, and realized my dick was hard again. I took it in my hand and slowly stroked it, pinching one of my nipples with my other hand. Eventually I shot a fourth load of creamy spunk. Finally, I stood up. I couldn't wear my clothes because they were all ripped and tattered up. What to do? I found a supply closet and pulled on a pair of overalls and a tee shirt that one of the guys had left in there. Dressed, I left the building and walked out onto the street. A car pulled up next to me and I saw Otis looking out at me from the passenger seat. The window of the passenger seat side was rolled down.

"Hey Big guy, need a ride?" Otis asked me, holding up my wedding band.

I gulped, stepped to the car, and climbed in the back seat. As we drove through the dark city streets Otis sucked my dick first in the back seat of the car.

A Boner Book

ABOUT THE AUTHOR

Christopher Trevor was born in July 1963 and grew up in New York City. As soon as he was old enough to know how he began writing fiction and has been writing gay erotic/fetish stories for the past ten to twelve years at this point. He became an avid reader as well from the time he knew how and reads everything from fiction, to non-fiction to biographies of interesting and unusual people, people who have made a difference or who have paved the way for others. Christopher attributes his writing artistic inspiration to artists such as Etienne, Tom of Finland, Tagame, The Hun, and most notably Joe T, who Christopher has had the pleasure of speaking with and even meeting over the last few years. Christopher states, "Joe T encouraged me to write about my fetish because I was embarrassed about it at the time. Joe T said that when we are embarrassed about something that makes it even more enticing somehow." Christopher totally agreed and never stopped writing in this genre. Erotic writers who inspired Christopher Trevor were: Tom Shaw (author of "That

Day at the Quarry), C.S. White (author of Big Sur), Larry Townsend (author of countless erotic novels), and Mason Powell (author of the classic story "The Brig.")

Christopher discovered that not only did he enjoy writing erotic tales but that after his first bondage experience he had a genuine flair for it. Writing to erotic oriented magazines about his first bondage experience truly opened the floodgates for Christopher where this style of writing is concerned. Christopher thanks the handsome and muscular "Greg" for that experience way back in time. Christopher took "Creative Writing" courses every semester during his high school years and while other friends of his stopped writing what they loved to write about as time went on Christopher never let a day go by when he didn't write something... "I feel that if I don't write every day I will die," Christopher has said many times over.

Foot fetish stories and all things related; spanking fetish, erotic shaving, muscle bondage, tickle torture, and hardcore stories are just a few of the areas of gay eroticism that Christopher enjoys writing about and inspiring in others as well. As one internet buddy said to Christopher where the black socks fetish is concerned, "Until I started talking with you I never gave a thought to my socks when I got dressed for work in the morning. Now when I pull my dress socks on every morning I get a chill up my spine."

Christopher is proud of the erotic effect he has on people...

Christopher Trevor is also the author of:

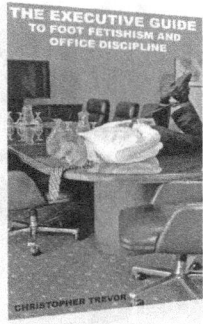

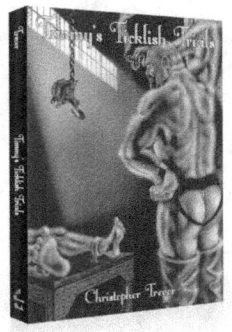

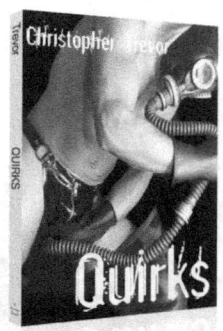